Who's Your Daddy?

LYNDA SANDOVAL

Simon Pulse
New York   London   Toronto   Sydney

*For Terri Farley, a talented author
and excellent travel buddy,
but most of all, my cherished friend.*

This book is a work of fiction. Any references to historical events, real people, or real locales are used fictitiously. Other names, characters, places, and incidents are the product of the author's imagination, and any resemblance to actual events or locales or persons, living or dead, is entirely coincidental.

SIMON PULSE

An imprint of Simon & Schuster Children's Publishing Division
1230 Avenue of the Americas, New York, NY 10020

Designed by Ann Zeak
The text of this book was set in Oranda BT.

Manufactured in the United States of America
First Simon Pulse edition month October 2004
2 4 6 8 10 9 7 5 3 1
Library of Congress Control Number 2003116407
ISBN 0-689-86440-X

one

★▉▉★▉▉★▉▉★

Here's what blows:

Sometimes, through no fault of your own, but based on who happened to bring you into the world, you become a social mutant with no foreseeable remedy beyond changing your identity and disappearing forever. How fair is that?

Take my best friend Meryl. Named after Meryl Streep, I suppose. But really, when you're sixteen it's just a weird name, and it makes no sense that she's named after Meryl Streep anyway because Meryl's parents don't even own a TV, much less patronize the theaters. *Meryl* Meryl, that is. Not Meryl Streep. I'm sure Ms. Streep's parents go to movies—seeing as how their daughter *stars* in them and they'd want to be supportive—and they probably have a TV, too. Probably a fifty-inch HDTV flat screen. Probably a gift from their daughter.

Whatever.

The point is, Meryl *Morgenstern*'s dad comes with the triple whammy mutant-making qualities of (1) he's the VP of discipline in our school, i.e., if you're a trouble-maker or a rebel, he knows it and you've probably spent quality time in his detention center, and (2) he's also the driver's ed teacher, so you can guarantee HIS daughter isn't going to get in the car with any of the guys, because he knows how incredibly bad they drive. Finally, (3) he's the assistant football coach, so none of the jocks want to piss him off.

Couple the triple whammy with the fact that Meryl's family is so anti–pop culture that you can mention the name BUFFY and Meryl's like, *blink, blink,* "Who?", and I can guarantee you the word DATE in Meryl's life refers solely to fruit.

Then there's Caressa Thibodoux, my other best friend, who has a few marks against her as well. First, she's the late-in-life daughter of a very famous, semi-retired blues musician from Louisiana and his third wife, who doesn't seem like she's much older than us but is probably fairly old, like in her latish thirties. I mean, I don't think Mr. Thibodoux totally robbed the cradle in a creepy way when they got together. Caressa's dad is the richest and most famous person in our town, even though, to us, he's just some old guy who comes down the stairs every now and then, in his bathrobe and these grandpa-looking slippers, to grab a piece of cold chicken from the fridge and stick his head into the family room to tell us to "keep it down."

Meaning the noise.

We can get a little loud.

Their house is the closest thing to a mansion in all of White Peaks, which is mostly made up of your typical Colorado mountain homes—cabins, the stone or cedar-sided types, the occasional A-frame or prefab. The Thibodoux house is sort of log-cabinesque, but it's the kind of place you'd move into if, say, you were Christie Brinkley and you survived a helicopter crash over the Rockies, had a romantic epiphany, and decided to stay west instead of moving back to your estate on Long Island.

Like, a log cabin *mansion*.

It has a portico and a recording studio. Need I say more?

Caressa's also some kind of reluctant musical prodigy and, at least in my mind, the girl most likely to blow this town and become someone famous (even if it's not in music) after we make it through the Seventh Circle of Hell which is White Peaks High School. (I swear, if one more adult tells me these are the best years of my life, I'm going to shave my head and tattoo a four-letter word on the back of my bare skull, and—oh yes—it will start with an *F*.)

To make matters worse, Caressa's also beautiful. The kind of breezy beautiful that makes high school guys dumber than they already are organically, what with all their blood rushing south on a regular basis. She's the kind of beautiful that's intimidating. Like, *Vogue* beautiful. Fly girl, J-Lo beautiful. But she doesn't even know it. So, you see, she's pretty well hosed in the guy department, despite what you might imagine. But think about it. A gorgeous, poised, rich, musically gifted daughter of a famous musician?

Yeah, the date thing? Not likely.

Not in high school, at least. Not in White Peaks, freakin' Colorado, for cripes sake. Mind you, Caressa *does* attract the attention of older guys, but like, have they *not* heard the term "jailbait" before? Please.

Then there's me, Lila Moreno. I have the lovely distinction of being the only daughter of our town's zero-tolerance-for-screwups police chief, and the little sister of four nosy, meddling brothers who intimidate every guy in town. Bad enough already, right? Well, sit back. It gets worse. Not only is my dad the aforementioned Intimidating Authority Figure, but—and I must cringe while I admit this part because the BLECH factor is SO off the scale—he's a hottie.

Yep, my dad. I mean, for an old guy.

He's a hottie, and he's a widower, and since that's a well-known fact, all the mothers, attached or otherwise, seem to become even dumber around my dad than the high school guys get around Caressa. Which sucks! I ask you, what guy in his right mind would want to date a girl when his own MOTHER has the hots for the girl's FATHER?

It's so gross! Really.

I mean, how much am I supposed to take?

For example, how would YOU like to go bra shopping with your FATHER, and then have the stupid bra lady pay more attention to him than to the fact that it's excruciatingly heinous to be browsing bras with (1) a man, who is (2) your father, in the first place?

Anyway, the whole bra thing? A psychic wound perhaps, and worth exploring later in my journal, but *so* not the point.

The point is that Meryl, Caressa, and I are White Peaks freaks, and there's nothing we can do about it except wait to grow up, move away, and forevermore lie about the identity of our fathers to any potential dates. Right?

HELLO! We're sixteen!

We have eons before we can blaze, and frankly, we wouldn't mind having a little guy action *before* the big exodus from White Peaks. Is that so much to ask?

It's not that we don't love our fathers. We do. But we are ostracized directly because of who they are, rather than who WE are, which is why we've come to affectionately refer to ourselves as the *"Who's Your Daddy?"* club.

Caressa made it up. She's creative that way.

My brother, Luke, claims the name has vague porno flick overtones, but (1) he shouldn't eavesdrop on us, and (2) I'm 99.9 percent positive he doesn't have any direct knowledge of the porn industry, because my dad would wholeheartedly thrash him if he did. So, how would he know?

Luke's my only brother still at home (thank God). He's a senior and a cretin to boot and, although he's got the high school girls snowed into believing he's as much of a hottie as our father (lemmings), the ugly truth is, Luke indulges in, well, gross bodily functions more often and louder than any human being I've ever had the misfortune to encounter in all of my sixteen years. He's no catch, trust me. And I will use this information against him if need be.

So, yeah, his opinion matters. Not.

Anyway, back to us.

My whole point (my teachers say I have a hard time getting to the point, *blah blah blah* whatever, so here goes) is that in the string of mediocre days and weeks that added up to our full-on mediocre freshman and sophomore years at White Peaks, no day was quite so bad as that particular day in September of our junior year.

You know, the day when all hell broke loose.

The whole thing actually started the summer before

my sophomore year. Bored one day, I found myself thumbing through some of my dad's training materials from a fraud and forgery conference he'd attended, and that's what gave me the idea.

Throughout tenth grade, I had gained quite a rep as somewhat of a groundbreaking entrepreneur in our school, using the knowledge I'd gained from my dad's info. Don't wig—it wasn't anything THAT illegal. It's not like I was floating checks or printing up phony money. My foray into the slightly illegal was really more of a public service, if you ask me. Teenagers are the silent oppressed, and my skills were an equally silent way to fight the oppression. Plus, we are given certain gifts in life, and I think it's almost a sin not to use what we receive.

My gift was this: I could, after studying a parental signature only once, perfectly forge said signature on an absentee excuse note, report card form, or what have you, and I would perform this valuable service for my fellow students at the bargain price of five dollars per John Hancock.

Really, I think I could've raised my prices to ten bucks a shot and people would've still flocked to me, but I didn't want to go all inflation-crazy on my peers.

I'd had such a good thing going.

It had almost made me popular (almost).

The whole reason I'd started the forgery service was because Dad had promised to match however much money I had saved when it came time for me to buy a car (which was NOW, but he kept ignoring that fact), and as a babysitter in White Peaks, I was firmly second string. I'd already stockpiled two grand from my, ah, business. Plus another thousand from my more legitimate pursuits, i.e., the occasional babysitting gig, extra chores, bribing my brothers. Three thousand bucks, with the promise of much more to come before all was said and done, because I was never hurting for clients when it came to forged parental signatures.

Until I got busted that day.

I won't go into detail about how it happened because it's a way ugly memory for me to relive. But it was mostly coincidence and pure bad luck. Suffice to say, questions were raised by key school administrators after a certain parent called claiming no knowledge of a note she'd supposedly provided, and one of my clients rolled on me.

Don't worry. He'll pay.

But that's basically how I ended up hanging out with Mr. Morgenstern on day one of my five-day, in-school suspension, stuck in a little jail-like cubicle stealing peeks at *US Weekly* which I'd smuggled in with my Biology II homework, and knowing that getting suspended was a freakin' cakewalk compared to the punishment my dad would dole out when I got home.

I just never thought he'd actually cancel my driver's license with the Department of Motor Vehicles and cut it up right there in front of me. I mean, this was my LICENSE. And not only that, but for the first time, I hadn't looked like a vacant-eyed, fashion-victim knuckle dragger in a photograph. Where's the justice? As if I wasn't already considered a freak of monster proportions, now I wouldn't be able to drive until I turned eighteen. He might as well have whipped out his Sig Sauer P220 and shot me dead right there on the Pergo floor.

He also restricted me from my social life for the rest of the semester, which was no punishment at all really considering I didn't HAVE a social life, but I didn't tell him that. The only real social contact I had was hanging out with Meryl and Caressa, which we refer to as "studying" in front of the parents, and Dad said I could continue that because it was, he thought, schoolwork-related.

I should've been happy to have pulled at least that off, but I wasn't. Not with my shiny, brand new, Colorado driver license sitting like confetti in the bottom of the trash can. Plus, my dad told me I would have to perform some sort of community service, but he hadn't decided what yet. Fine with me, because I didn't want to know.

I spent the dinner hour sullenly pushing my food around my plate and trying my best to ignore Luke's smirks while simultaneously wanting to kill him. I needed to get out of the house and let off steam, so thank God I was still allowed to "study" with my friends. I think my dad was sick of the tension in the house too, so he was more than happy to sequester himself in the dining room after dinner to avoid us.

Not wanting to push my luck, I dutifully cleaned up the kitchen, then hooked my backpack over my shoulder and stood in the entrance to the dining room. My dad was frowning over a bunch of case files spread out on the table in front of him, looking vaguely like Esai Morales from *NYPD Blue*, with a little more distinguished gray at the temples.

I cleared my throat. "I'm going to Caressa's to study."

Dad's arms remained braced on the edge of the table, but his eyes raised from the files. "Is the kitchen clean?"

"Yes."

"How are you going to get there?"

Rub it in, why don't you? I thought, fighting not to roll my eyes. "My bike," I said, attempting to sound stoic and martyr-esque, hoping the guilt would eat him alive when I made the front page of the *Peaks Picayune* after getting munched by a wild animal or kidnapped by a freaky mountain man with a meth lab in his basement. "Or I'll walk."

"Don't be silly. It's cold."

Not to mention the bears and mountain lions and freaky mountain dudes with bad tooth-to-tattoo ratios, but whatever.

"Have your brother take you." He turned toward the family room and called, "Luke?"

I shifted on my feet, but knew I was in too much trouble already to pitch a fit. Truth was, I'd rather end up hypothermic or mauled by a bear than ride in the car with my smug, smirking brother and his "I told you so" attitude. I clamped my lips together and said nothing.

Luke stuck his head into the dining room, all freakin' zoned out from a dose of *The Man Show* or *Jackass* or some other equally brain-numbing anti-stimuli—just what he needed. "Huh?"

"Drive your sister to Caressa's."

"But, Dad—"

"Now."

The air of pissed-offedness hung thick and ominous in the house, premonitions of butt-kickings to come, so Luke shut his trap, too. He snagged his keys off the hook by the door with an angry swipe and glared at me. "Come on, Felon," he growled under his breath.

I punched him in the arm. "Don't call me that."

He ignored me, instead spreading his thumbs and forefingers and placing them tip to tip to make a box. "*Forgery for Fun and Profit,* by Lila Moreno. I can just see the book cover."

"Bite me, buttwipe," I said, pushing past him into the cold, dark, Rocky Mountain night. The elk had been bugling earlier in the day—a sound I'd always loved, like whale song—but now the black night fell silent.

Thankfully, so did Luke. I had expected him to taunt

me about getting busted, but instead he drove to Caressa's with Disturbed pounding and vibrating from the stereo speakers, drumming his fingers on the wheel. He'd left his window open to the thirty-five-degree air, though, because he knew being cold annoyed me, and he loved to annoy me. I just concentrated on the flashes of gold from the aspen trees between the black of the pines along the sides of the road.

When he screeched to a stop in the portico, I leapt from the car and muttered, "Caressa will bring me home," trying not to let my teeth chatter.

He snorted. "Like I offered to pick you up."

I slammed the door, wanting to stick out my tongue but deciding that was SO seventh grade. Why did I let him get me so riled up? Luke wasn't that bad of a brother overall. He was just a guy. What can I say? Guys often suck, as a rule, and brothers are the worst. We used to be pals until . . . I wasn't sure when it had changed. I think it had something to do with me entering high school and immediately being shuffled into the loser corral. God forbid Luke would stick up for me. Apparently the attentions of a certain cheerleading überskank were more important than blood relations to

His Shallow Highness. But I set his lameness aside, glad to be with my friends at last.

They say misery loves company, and if so I was in for my first bit of luck. As it turned out, I wasn't the only one who'd suffered a heinous day (although we all agreed, due to the license thing, I was in first place on the suck scale). Meryl had been trying out for the debate team, but in the semifinal round that afternoon, she'd tanked in a big way when most of her topics dealt with the worst of all possible things—movies and television. Bummed didn't come close to describing her mood. Meryl is so smart, we were bummed for her, too.

Caressa, on the other hand, had what most people would consider a good day—on the surface. Even though she hadn't formally auditioned, she'd been cast for the lead in the spring musical—*Beauty and the Beast*. The only problem was, Caressa didn't *want* the lead. She had no desire whatsoever to sing—it was the whole totally "doing whatever your parents had done" thing. Blech.

The coolio-factor of playing Belle and wearing kick-butt costumes weren't even enough to drag Caressa out of depressionville. She had joined the theater club because she likes *makeup,* not singing. No, she LOVES makeup—worships at the temple of Sephora.com on a regular basis, if you want the whole truth. She wanted to work behind the scenes, doing makeup and costuming for the various productions. But, of course, having Lehigh Thibodoux, aka Tibby Lee, for a father meant, once again, Caressa got jammed. The theater club sponsor, Mr. Cabbiatti, who is a celebrity-wannabe to an epic degree, couldn't pass up the publicity opportunity. Now all the girls who wanted to play Belle were angry with Caressa for getting a part she didn't even want, and Caressa was angry because she just wanted to put makeup on the beast. Go figure!

We were all sitting around that night, painting each other's toenails, complaining about our parents and our horrid luck, and bemoaning the fact that homecoming loomed and none of us had dates or even prospects.

Surprising? No. Depressing? Uh, yes.

Fiona Apple was playing on the stereo, because we wanted to feed our already depressed moods, and so far, no directives from Mr. Thibodoux to "keep it down."

Caressa was bent low over my feet painting my toenails with this sweet OPI shade she'd just bought, "I'm

Not Really a Waitress." It's kind of a red with sparkly gold in it. I had a hard time deciding between that and another shade from OPI's European collection called, "Amster-Damsel in Distress," but the gold shimmer in "Waitress" really won me over.

Caressa always has the best makeup.

Anyway, she was concentrating on my pinky toe, left foot, when out of nowhere Meryl goes, "We need to change our lives. Homecoming is on the autumnal equinox this year."

As though those two comments were related.

"Huh," Caressa and I said in unison, not knowing what type of response was appropriate to the equinox-announcement-slash-life-change directive. I mean, we'd been talking about how much our lives sucked, but the equinox? All I knew for sure was that homecoming had been rescheduled and would commence the following Tuesday night. Yes, a freakin' Tuesday, if you can believe that lunacy. The switch was the school district's brilliant solution to avoiding a big, heinous snowstorm expected on Friday.

Whatever. Tuesday, Friday. Equinox Schmequinox. You could only complain for so long, and Meryl always launched interesting conversations, so we went with it. That's one cool thing about having a friend who's completely Laura Ingalls Wilder-ish out of touch with the American entertainment scene (or any entertainment scene, really)—she has tons of time to read stuff the rest of the high school universe would pass up in favor of this week's installment of *The Real World*. She's always popping off bits of useless but nevertheless pretty interesting trivia.

Meryl also works a couple of nights a week at the local metaphysical shop downtown, since Mr. Morgenstern put the giant kibosh on her first choice job at Blockbuster. Frankly, I think the metaphysical shop is a much better place to work anyway. It always smells good in there from the flickering candles and essential oils, and the tinkling bells and gurgling serenity fountains are soothing.

Compare that atmosphere to one of bright, corporate clone paint, fluorescent lights, zit-faced, overzealous assistant managers, and nonstop video background noise, and the choice is obvious. Plus, at Inner Power, she only has to work with the two way-mellow women who own the shop rather than all the mouth-breathing

vidiots who work at Blockbuster, and she [...]
kinds of sweet stuff about, well, metaph[...]

"Since we're not going," Meryl cont[...]
should all spend the night at Caressa's and have a du[...]
supper."

That made both Caressa and I blink up at her in confusion.

"If it's okay with your parents, of course," she
added, glancing over at Caressa.

"It always is." Caressa shrugged. Her parents, as a
rule, were totally cool about stuff like that.

"A dumb supper?" I interjected, just as Caressa and I
exchanged a look. "You mean, like something we all
hate? Great idea, Meryl," I said, not bothering to hide
my sarcasm. "Brilliant. That would really cheer us up."

"No, goof. It's a tradition that dates back to seventeenth-
century England. It's a midsummer's eve custom—"

"Yeeeeeah, newsflash. It's not summer," I pointed
out, even though it *had* to be obvious, even for a person
who didn't watch the evening news. Hello, snowstorm!

"Still," Meryl said, unfazed by my sarcasm. "I think
it's adaptable. It's all about our intent." She shrugged.
"If they can hold homecoming on a school night, I figure

can host a dumb supper on the equinox rather than midsummer's eve."

She had a point.

"What do we have to do?" Caressa asked, her eyes glowing with curiosity that mirrored how I felt.

"Well, there are lots of details, but in general we have to hold a silent dinner that starts at midnight, with only black linens and total darkness. Well, except for candles. We have to make and serve everything backward, and—oh, it's a long story. I'll explain it all later." She flipped her hand. "The point is, it's supposed to help us predict who we'll marry, but since we're only sixteen, I'm thinking it will help us predict who we might date instead. What do you think?"

"Is it reliable?" asked Caressa.

Meryl quirked her mouth to the side. "Well, it's been going on since the sixteen hundreds. It can't be *all* stupid." She looked from one of us to the other. "So?"

"I'm game," I said. Anything to take my mind off how much my life blew major chunks.

"Me, too," said Caressa.

Meryl's face spread into a huge smile. "Then it's a date."

"A date? Well—" I said, "even if this dinner turns out to actually *be* dumb, at least we'll each be able to say we had ONE date this year."

We all laughed, but the truth was, we couldn't wait. I could hear it in my own breathlessness, in the equally nervous and psyched laughter of my two best friends. It gave us something to look forward to, and boy, did we need it.

Little did we know how this harmless, losers'-alternative-to-homecoming, dumb supper would end up changing our entire lives.

two

■■■■*■■*

FROM: MerylM@Morgensternfamily.com

TO: LawBreakR@hipgirlnet.org, Lipstickgrrrrl@hip-girlnet.org

SUBJECT: DUMB SUPPER, print and read!!!!!

TIME: 4:11:11 A.M., MST

*****CARESSA AND LILA, PRINT THIS EMAIL FOR FUTURE REFERENCE*****

Meryl's Rules for the dumb supper

L&C—

I've read up on various dumb supper traditions, and I ended up incorporating a little of this and a little of that to make the ritual personalized for US. :-) First, Lila, I think it's so special that you're willing to have your mother as our "spirit guest." I'm glad it didn't freak you out that we needed to invite someone who'd passed on.

Here is what I need each of you to bring: Lila—white gel pens and black notecards are VERY important. Also, please buy the following items at the party store:

1. black paper plates
2. black napkins
3. black plastic forks, spoons, knives
4. black tablecloth
5. black fabric (to shroud the "spirit chair" for your mom)
6.black cups
7.black and white votive candles (lots of black, one white)
8.black serving bowls

You'll note the theme: BLACK. Holler if you have trouble finding any of this, and I'll help.

Caressa, you're already donating your house (along with stuff like lighters, etc.), but I'm going to make you in charge of getting the food together. The nine food items we decided on for our feast, in backward order, are:

1. Sara Lee cheesecake (dessert)
2. Turtle brownies (dessert)

3. Cheeze Whiz (cheese course)

4. Potato chips (side dish)

5. Rotisserie chicken (main course)

6. Celery with peanut butter (salad course)

7. Cup-a-Soup (soup course)

8. Taquitos (appetizer)

9. Fresca (beverage)

All of these items are available at Safeway, but you probably knew that.

As for me, I'm going to bring the ritual items we need, like sage sticks to purify the room and our chosen divination tools:

Lila: black scrying mirror

Caressa: brass singing bowl

Me: rosaline crystal ball

Here's how the night will unfold:

Lila, I'll pick you up. When we get to Caressa's, we'll prepare the food, and I'll purify the feast room with sage sticks. We will also write our prayer/wishes on the black notecards. These prayer/wishes should have something to do with the guys we each hope to find.

At EXACTLY midnight, we will all enter the feast room and set our prayer/wish cards at our designated places. After that, Caressa and I will begin carrying items in to set up the table. Remember, ABSOLUTELY NO TALKING, LAUGHING, ETC. in the feast room. Caressa, you and I have to carry each item in together, with your hand on one side and mine on the other. It will take a while, but we can make it go faster if we plan it all out beforehand, maybe even rehearse. Here's the order:

1. Tablecloth
2. Candles
3. Spirit chair shroud
4. Plates
5. Napkins
6. Silverware
7. Cups
8. Food items, in order

Once all the food is on the table, Caressa and I will enter the feast room backward and sit in the chairs backward. Lila, you'll come in backward and lay your hands on the back of the spirit chair. Welcome your mother's spirit (SILENTLY!) to our supper. Light the white votive candle and place it on the plate in front of her chair, then light one black votive candle for each of us and place them, one by one, on the plates in front of us. Take a seat backward on your chair, Lila, and then we'll eat. Dessert to appetizers, the way it should be in REAL LIFE.

YUM!

At the end of the meal, we will, one by one, pull our prayer/wishes out from under our plates, and we'll burn them with our black votive candles.

The prediction part goes like this: whichever guy each of us sees FIRST at the end of this ritual will be the guy we're supposed to date. What fun, huh?????? Junior prom, here we come! Let me know if you have any questions.

L&K, Meryl

FROM: LawBreakR@hipgirlnet.org
TO: MerylM@Morgensternfamily.com,
Lipstickgrrrrl@hipgirlnet.org
SUBJECT: re: DUMB SUPPER, print and read!!!!!
TIME: 6:29:33 A.M., MST

Mer:

A) What are you doing up at four in the morning??????

B) Are you sure I can get black stuff at the party

store? Won't it have something written on it like, "Over the Hill," or something? If it does say "Over the Hill" or "Happy Halloween," is it still okay?

C) I did think it was slightly creepazoid at first that we had to invite a dead relative, but I got to thinking it will be pretty cool having my mom "participate" in finding me a boyfriend. I'm sure she would've given me help/advice if she was still here. So, no worries. I'm not freaked.

D) The menu sounds great!

E) I CAN'T WAIT FOR NEXT TUESDAY!!!!! I agree, junior prom, HERE WE COME!

<SWAK>

—Lila

FROM: MerylM@Morgensternfamily.com
TO: LawBreakR@hipgirlnet.org, Lipstickgrrrrl@hipgirlnet.org
SUBJECT: re: DUMB SUPPER, print and read!!!!!
TIME: 7:37:03 A.M., MST

Lila:

To answer your questions and comment on your comments:

A) I couldn't sleep—excited!

B) Yes, you can find black stuff at the party store. NO, it won't all have "Over the Hill" or "Happy Halloween" on it, and don't buy it if it does.

C) I'm glad re: your mom. It really was our only choice, since neither Caressa nor I have lost anyone we love, so it's good you're okay with it. I think it's really nice to have your mom there, too. In spirit.

D) The food does sound yummy! We should be chefs.

E) Me neither!

L&K,

Meryl

FROM: Lipstickgrrrrl@hipgirlnet.org
TO: LawBreakR@hipgirlnet.org,
MerylM@Morgensternfamily.com
SUBJECT: re: DUMB SUPPER, print and read!!!!!
TIME: 7:45:47 A.M., MST

Meryl and Lila—

This sounds like SO MUCH FUN! I told my parents we were studying old English customs for school, and they not only bought it, they agreed to go into Denver, see a show, and stay in a hotel so we can have "an authentic experience" without interruption. I felt guilty for the LWL at first, then I realized we really ARE studying old English customs, and although it's not EXACTLY for school, it is to find boyfriends. Boyfriends are at school, boyfriends will make going to school BETTER, so by a few degrees of separation, we are studying old English customs for school.

Poof, guilt gone.

I will do my shopping ASAP. Lila, since you don't have a car or a license (NO OFFENSE—HUGS!!), and you're grounded, you can give me your list and $$$ if you want and I'll shop for you. Let me know. Tuesday can't come soon enough for me! I really feel like we'll all have dates to the Junior Prom!

—Love, C

FROM: LawBreakR@hipgirlnet.org
TO: MerylM@Morgensternfamily.com,
Lipstickgrrrrl@hipgirlnet.org
SUBJECT: re: DUMB SUPPER, print and read!!!!!
TIME: 8:40:02 A.M., MST

At 7:45:47 A.M., MST, [Lipstickgrrrrl@hipgirlnet.org] wrote:

Lila, since you don't have a car or a license (NO OFFENSE—HUGS!!), and you're grounded, you can give me your list and $$$ if you want and I'll shop for you. Let me know.

UGH, that was HARSH-O-RAMA, Caressa! :-Z But yes, I'll give you my money and you can hook me up. Thanks.
—Carless Lila, living in hell

"No way."

I gaped at my father, bug-eyed with horror, mouth hanging open, so totally NOT believing what I was hearing. This arbitrary decision of his could very well ruin my life! *Why* couldn't he remember way, way, way back to when he was my age and, just this once, show a little compassion for my plight? I know Grandma and Grandpa Moreno snapped a big ol' knot in his butt on a regular basis when he was a teenager, but he seemed to be suffering from some sort of parental amnesia that completely wiped out that memory.

I was halfway convinced that parents got secret monetary kickbacks from the government for conveniently forgetting how it was to be a teenager and making their own kids' lives hell, perpetuating some big, ugly cycle. I can tell you, when I have kids someday, I won't put them through this trauma. But, hey, I might NEVER have kids. I attended health class, just like every other girl at WPHS, and I'm pretty clear about the fact that, in order for one to eventually get to the point of GIVING BIRTH, one must first come into CONTACT with the opposite sex. I hadn't even reached step one. And now it looked like I might not.

"W-what do you mean, no way?" I sputtered to my father at last. My throat tightened as I fought to hold back the full-on rant that wanted to erupt. As a result, my voice came out sounding like Minnie Mouse if she were choking on a Jolly Rancher. "You said I was allowed to study with the girls," I squeaked. "We're going to be studying."

"Study in the evening and plan accordingly so you can come home when you're done."

"But—"

"Lila." He dipped his chin in that annoying way that made me feel like I was being charged with a crime and had about an ice cube's chance in hell of getting off by reason of insanity (or any other reason). "I know you operate under the assumption that I was born yesterday, my dear daughter, but no one studies at midnight."

He had a point. I hadn't thought that through. And I hated when he called me "my dear daughter," because it always meant he was on to me. He never called my brothers "my dear sons."

"Not to mention, you're grounded," he added unnecessarily.

"But—"

"Which means, no overnights. And no manipulating me to get out of your punishment this time."

Dangit. He left me without grounds for an argument. I *did* have a reputation for trying to, shall we say, finesse my way out of consequences, but hey, I was good at it. All that aside, the burning question remained: how could I miss the dumb supper? It was the one and only event, other than the prospect of moving away from White Peaks forEVER, that gave me hope for the future.

"B-but, Dad—" I couldn't think of a good angle with which to state my case, so I resorted to stomping my foot and regressing to fifth grade. "It's not fair!"

"*Callaté.*"

Uh-oh. He only ordered me to shut my trap *in Spanish* when I'd pushed him to the very edge of his patience. I pressed my lips together but continued to scowl. My chest rose and fell with fury. It flooded through my veins like liquid fire, causing my body temperature to spike. "But—"

"But, *nada*." Dad's face hardened in that all-too-familiar stubborn-cop way. His voice got meaner, too. "Lila Jane Moreno, read my lips. You are not staying over at Caressa's on homecoming night. Now, drop it." His hand sliced out to the side, palm down. "I had a long day at work and I want a little peace and quiet."

I rolled my eyes so hard, my contact lens curled up on the edge. Oh, sure. HIS heinous day mattered, but my entire awful existence didn't. I knew it was useless to argue, so instead I whirled in my stocking feet, planning on a dramatic, Oscar-worthy exit at the very LEAST. Instead, I crashed facefirst into my brother's chest, smashing my nose to the side hard enough to make my eyes water.

"Shut your hole," I snapped, grabbing onto my nose in case it started spurting blood.

He spread his arms. "I didn't say anything, hormone queen!"

I shoved him aside as my eyes watered harder. "Shut it anyway!"

"Lila," I heard my dad call out, "don't say 'shut your hole.' It's vulgar."

"Oh, yeah!" I hollered, spinning to face them. "But he can call me hormone queen! That's gender harassment! I'm a persecuted minority in this family! I'm calling the ACLU or . . . or the Lifetime Channel, or something!"

"Lila, I mean it. I've had enough."

"Bite me," I whispered under my breath as I stomped away, immediately feeling a stab of guilt for having said it. Sure, I was cranked off at my dad for this latest bout of persecution, but as fathers went, USUALLY he was an okay guy. Still. I had every right to be angry. My life kept getting worse, no matter how hard I struggled to make it better.

I tried to earn car money babysitting, but everyone wanted the peppy little cheerleaders (a monopoly, mark my words). I subsequently found another creative way to earn fundage, but NO. One of my chickens**t clients had to go and rat me out, the hypocritical dirtbag. Then, instead of Dad recognizing my entrepreneurial genius, he—and all the other adults—saw me as some sort of at-risk youth. A juvenile delinquent.

My license? Gone.

The car-matching fund? *Pffft.*

Now, just when I had the chance to, perhaps, find a way out of my bottom-feeder social cesspool? DENIED. Again.

SO wrong.

I pounded my way up the steps but exercised enough self-restraint to avoid slamming my bedroom door off its hinges. Dad hated that more than any other annoying thing, and there was no sense pushing my luck at this stage of the game. I threw myself facedown on my bed until my pounding heart had regulated itself and my breathing returned to normal. I never could think straight when I was flipping out. When my mind had cleared, I pondered the dilemma as rationally as possible.

Here's the point my father did not grasp: I COULD NOT MISS THIS EVENT!!! Fate had brought the idea of the dumb supper into our lives. I was sure of it. What if, by missing it, I annoyed the fate gods enough to assure I would never have a single date? Years would drag by, and I'd wind up as a career virgin by age twenty-seven. Life would be OVER for me. Future teenagers would study me in history class, in an effort to avoid repeating my mistakes. Couldn't he see the horrible gravity of the situation?!?!?!?

Okay, so he didn't actually *know* what fate had planned for us that night—he thought we were studying—and I might be overreacting slightly with the career virgin scenario (the jury was still out on that one). But I couldn't exactly spell out the-whole-truth-and-nothing-but for the guy. Hello, GROUNDED! Remember that? Thanks to his cruel and unusual punishment, I HAD to use the studying spiel. He'd left me no other choice.

I frowned so hard it gave me a headache behind my eyes. Unfair, unfair, unfair. All of it—from being the only girl in a family of five creepy males, to having my cash cow chopped into hamburgers (ew!), to being grounded, to missing the equinox. ACKKKK!!!! My own FATHER would see more homecoming action than I would. In fact, I'd be the ONLY Moreno stuck at home that night!

How much worse could things get?

I was 0-for-3 on homecoming dates in my thus-far illustrious high school career. Now I'd be on house arrest while Luke escorted Supertramp to the festivities and my FATHER trolled from party to party with the rest of the cops. The heavy police presence was my dad's proactive solution to avoiding a rash of alcohol-related teen deaths that would land White Peaks (and him) on the front page of *The Denver Post*. Of course, I'd never wind up in the *Post*, because I'd be stuck at home surfing bad digital cable like all the rest of the losers, and ALL of it simply because I'd found a profitable way to fill a sorely needed market demand. (Who? Me? Bitter? What makes you think that?)

Wait one freakin' second.

The realization hit me like an electrical jolt.

I was missing my own point. Dad would be at *work*.

I lifted my face from my pillow, hope bubbling up out of my pool of pissed-offedness and making me smile like the Grinch. What the old guy didn't know couldn't possibly hurt him, right? Meaning my dad, not the Grinch. If he wasn't even *home*, how would he know whether I'd gone to Caressa's or not?

Relief flooded through me now that a viable idea had percolated in my brain. I sat up, then scuffed my way across the room to my computer, booted it up, and checked my buddy list for the presence of Meryl and

Caressa (both there). I quickly sent them a chat invite, then drummed my fingers on the desktop until two identical musical "blings" alerted me that they'd entered the private chat room.

Lipstickgrrrrl:

Hey, Lila. Whazzup?

MerylM:

Hi guys.

Lipstickgrrrrl:

Hi MM!

LawBreakR:

First off, MY LIFE SUCKS!!!!!!!!!!!!!!!!!! Sucks, I tell you!

Lipstickgrrrrl:

Why?! What happened??

MerylM:

Why?

LawBreakR:

My freakin' dad told me I couldn't come to your house on homecoming night, Caressa, that's why.

Lipstickgrrrrl:

R U kidding? :-O

MerylM:

You HAVE to come!! :-(((((

LawBreakR:

Oh, don't worry, Mer. I'm coming. I don't care WHAT he says. For God's sake, I'm SIXTEEN!!!!!!!! It's not like I'm a CHILD. :-P

MerylM:

Wait a minute. Lila, don't make things WORSE for yourself! Your dad will KILL you if you disobey him.

LawBreakR:

Life couldn't possibly BE worse, Mer!!!!! I am NOT, I repeat NOT, missing the dumb supper!!!!!!!!!!!!!! Just listen to my idea.

Lipstickgrrrrl:

Don't do anything crazy. :-Z

LawBreakR:

Sheesh, you wimp girls. I'm not going to run away or kill him in his bed or anything. If I was going to whack anyone while he slept, it would be Luke. Believe me. I do have a foolproof plan, though.

MerylM:

Uh-oh.

Lipstickgrrrrl:

What kind of plan?

LawBreakR:

He (Dad) works that night, because of homecoming, remember? He won't be home until three or four A.M. I'll sneak out and be back before he realizes I'm gone. It's perf!!!!!!!! :-D

MerylM:

UGH, I don't know. That makes my stomach nervous. He'll end up hating all of us. :-\

Lipstickgrrrrl:

Lila, yeah. Meryl's right. Just forget it. You'll end up grounded until you're thirty, and this time you won't be able to see us, either. We can reskedge.

LawBreakR:

NO WAY!!!!!!!!!!!!!!!!!!!! We HAVE to do it on the equinox! I just feel it!

Lipstickgrrrrl:

It's our INTENT, right, Meryl? We can do it anytime.

MerylM:

Right.

LawBreakR:

I will NOT put my life on hold just because I got unfairly busted for creating an empire out of forged siggys! Donald Trump would probably give me my own company if I was HIS kid.

MerylM:

But, you're NOT Trump's kid. You're the POLICE CHIEF'S kid. GRASP THE DIFFERENCE, LILA! What if you get caught??

LawBreakR:

[scoff] I WON'T get caught, and anyway, my life already blows. Even if I did, what could he possibly do to make it worse?????????

Lipstickgrrrrl:

Famous last words.

LawBreakR:

Ha-freakin'-ha. I will not live under these conditions! I'm a human being! An American. I have RIGHTS!!!

MerylM:

Actually, as a teenager, not many. Not even as an American teenager, which we can discuss further sometime if you're interested in the parameters of the law. And the bust was kind of a big deal. No offense!!! I'm not discounting your unique talent for forgery. :-)

Lipstickgrrrrl:

LOL! Rights. [snort] You're so dramatic, Lila. Maybe YOU should be in the stupid play instead of me.

LawBreakR:

I can't act. I can't sing. Be quiet. And I don't want to hear about my teenage rights, Meryl, or the lack thereof. I'm depressed enough as it is. WAHHHH!! You guys are NOT giving me the props I need. :-(((((Crap, gotta blaze. [sigh] He's bellowing that dinner's ready, LIKE I want to eat. Anyway. I need to fly under the radar big time until next Tuesday, so I can pull off my plan to sneak out—AND I WILL!! So, color me scarce. Hit me on email if you need me or talk to me at school. Later, chicas!

Lipstickgrrrrl:

Ciao, bellas. ((((((((((Lila))))))))))

MerylM:

TTYL! (((((((((Lila)))))))))

LawBreakR:

Thx, GFs. Hugs back! (((((((((((U2))))))))))))))) (not the band. Duh.)

I signed out of the chat room and bounded down the stairs, wondering why Meryl and Caressa were so afraid of me getting busted. PLEASE. I could handle this. Had they no faith at all? My stomach growled, alerting me to the fact that I actually *was* hungry after all. I wasn't surprised, though. Having a scheme in the works always gave me an appetite.

My older brothers' voices carried into the living room as I walked through it, reminding me that this was the night we were all together for dinner. I already knew, of course, but I'd forgotten. We only got together about once a month with the way everyone's schedules conflicted. My two oldest brothers, Nathan Jr. and Gilbert, were cops down on the flats, for the Aurora and Denver Police Departments, respectively. David was in the DPD academy. Luke was a Police Explorer here in White Peaks, aka a member of the junior narc squad. (Puke.)

As you can see, I was outnumbered by all these freakin' GI Joes, not to mention being the only girl in the family and the only kid who would rather DIE than become a cop. Still, for better or for worse, they were my *family*. Now that Nate and Gil and David were out of the house, I didn't mind seeing them in small doses, although their law enforcement conversations were mindnumbing at best. Luke, of course, remained a hemorrhoid on the hinter regions of my life, and I was counting the days until the screen door hit him in the crack on the way out of the house for good. Thank God he was a senior.

For once, I didn't scowl at the testosterone-overloaded atmosphere that typified life with my dad and brothers, nor did I intentionally rebel against everything they believed in. This was my chance. I'd show them all just what a perfect angel I could be, and soon Dad would stop watching me like a felon on parole. If I could really lay the innocent stuff on thick, next Tuesday's plan would be cake—angel food, of course.

I strutted into the kitchen and shocked each of my brothers with a kiss on the cheek (except Luke—I gave him a wet willy when my dad's back was turned, which earned me a backhanded smack in the gut, which earned him my middle finger, and so on), then took my seat and spread my napkin neatly on my lap. I even paid attention to my posture.

Dad set a bubbling casserole dish on the patrol car–shaped trivets some badge-bunny single mom had made him a couple years ago, in an effort to snare him. The way they chased him was truly gagworthy, let me tell you. I wanted to date, sure, but I made a silent vow that I'd never be THAT desperate for a guy, even if I DID get to be as old as The Moms and remained single.

TRIVETS?! Please.

I leaned up and peered into the dish, launching into my *Operation: Lie Low* plan. "Yum," I said, with a combination of sincerity and enthusiasm. "Looks great, Dad. What is it?"

My dad blinked twice in my direction, taking his time to answer. The complete one-eighty turnaround in my attitude had clearly thrown him. His gaze narrowed suspiciously. "It's chicken spaghetti casserole."

I didn't even lecture him about what excessive carbs would do to the body of a man his age. HELLO, LOVE HANDLES! (A scary misnomer, if you ask me.) Instead, I smiled sweetly. "Can I have seconds?"

He raised one brow in disbelief or doubt, I wasn't sure which. My brothers had fallen silent during the exchange—which was, admittedly, quite un-ME-like— and they all stared at me with mistrust. I held my breath and prayed none of them would call me on it.

"You haven't even had firsts," Dad said.

"It just looks *that* good," I said, in this completely altruistic Mother Teresa tone of voice. I impressed MYSELF, I have to tell you.

Luke was the first to front me off. He rolled his eyes and launched into these exaggerated gagging sounds. I kicked him under the table, and he kicked me back. Hard.

Okay, so I'd laid it on a little thick, I admitted to myself, rubbing the rapidly growing knot on my shin. Still, by the time we'd all been served, the boys had launched into yet another lobotomizing cop conversation about probable cause or the latest chase policy, *blah blah blah*. I peered around unobtrusively, noting that Dad's focus had already shifted ever so slightly from me to them. One full week of this I'm-a-perfect-naive-Jessica-Simpson-angel schtick, and I'd be off the paternal radar screen completely. It so rocked.

I took a bite of the casserole—which actually *was* dang yummy—and chewed to hide my smug smile. I hated to boast, but I had this whole gig SO totally bagged. I may not want to follow in Dad's footsteps like all my cows-in-the-chute brothers had (vomitous thought), but you didn't grow up as a cop's daughter without picking up a few stealth-maneuver tricks along the way. If I do say so myself (and I DO), I excelled at stealth, and this week would prove it.

Next Tuesday night's escape-the-house plot? No sweat. And, the dumb supper? I was SO there.

three

* ■ ■ * ■ ■ * ■ ■ *

My homecoming-night escape was going perfectly according to plan until Luke and Mattress Girl unexpectedly returned to our house just as I was climbing out my window. Murphy's Law. He must've forgotten the dictionary his girlfriend needed in order to understand the most banal of conversations. *(Banal: drearily commonplace and often predictable; trite.* Surely, she could grasp the meaning of THAT word.)

The sweep of his headlights across my body scared the living crap out of me, and I froze in mid-dangle, my fingers cramped around the windowsill. I'd chosen to climb out the window rather than leave the old-fashioned way because it meant I could (1) leave my stereo on and (2) lock my door from the inside, so anyone who checked would think I was still home, sleeping away to my music like usual.

It was pitch dark out, but there I hung, trapped in the glare of the headlights, like some hardened crim scaling the wall of a prison while the searchlights moved over his orange-clad form. For several finger-destroying moments, I didn't move. I waited until Luke had disappeared inside the house, then jumped way too many feet from my window ledge to the ground.

OOF!

My landing knocked the wind out of me, so I hid facedown in the wild rosebush to catch my breath—which was NOT fun, let me tell you. Ever heard of freakin' thorns?

Luke's bubbleheaded wench of a girlfriend stood outside next to the idling car the whole time, smoking a cigarette. I kept an eye on her, just in case she was stupid enough to drop the smoldering cigarette on the ground and start a forest fire, but—miracle of miracles—she didn't.

I waited until she'd safely stowed her ciggy butt in a Coke can inside the car, then I took in a deep now-or-never breath. Teeth clenched, I low-crawled across our property until I reached the grove of aspen trees on the edge of the woods. Meryl would be waiting for me in her überancient, turquoise Volvo station wagon on the other side of the ridge.

I don't know what brought Luke and Miffany (I am not making that name up, sadly enough) home, but I needed to get to Meryl before they drove by, saw Meryl, put two and two together, and ruined the whole night. Meryl's ride wasn't exactly the blend-in sort. I usually loved the Volvo, but right now I was wishing her parents had bought her a maroon Subaru Outback station wagon, aka the National Car of White Peaks, which would have virtually disappeared into the landscape; there were so many of them.

I cast one more glance over my shoulder at the edge of the aspens, then stood up and crashed my way through the woods as if the Blair Witch was after me. Tree branches tore at my hair and clothing as I ran, and I fell not once, but three times. Hey, it was dark. What can I say? I had my camping headlamp clamped to my skull, but I couldn't risk turning it on. Our neighborhood gets so dark, any light source, no matter how small, shines through the trees like a million candle-power spot. So, I stumbled, ran, fell, and felt my way over the ridge to safety. I just prayed there were no bears or mountain lions lying in wait, with a huge hankering for a snack of freaked-out human.

Relief rushed through me when I caught a glimpse of Meryl's big ugly car, circa 1970-something, idling in the distance. I picked up speed, but tripped a few feet outside the car, launching myself airborne and landing facedown on the front window. OUCH.

Meryl jumped half a mile, letting out a little shriek; then she reached over and unlocked the passenger door with a shaky hand.

I peeled my aching body off the hood and hurled myself into the car, checking behind us before hunkering down in the seat.

"You scared me!"

"You knew I was coming," I whispered, for no logical reason. It wasn't like Luke and Friends had bionic hearing.

"Yes, but I didn't know you'd pull the bug-splattering-on-the-windshield routine."

"I didn't mean to. I tripped. Luke and his blowup play pal came home and almost caught me climbing out my window." I whipped another panicked glance behind us. "In fact, you need to step on it. They could come around the curve at any moment and our dinner plans will be screwed."

"Oh no!" Meryl, usually a careful driver, got caught up in the excitement or the urgency or something. She made like a Spy Kid on crack, spinning her wheels and chucking gravel in an arc behind us as she peeled out. "Why'd you cut it so close?"

"I didn't mean to! Luke came back to the house at ten P.M. for some reason. Why would he do that? He must've forgotten something, like his brain."

"What if he checked your bedroom?"

"Why would he?" I didn't want to think about it. "Besides, I left the door locked."

"Locked? From the inside?"

I nodded.

"That's why you climbed out the window?"

I nodded again.

She paused. "Uh, Lila? How are you going to get back in?"

I turned to stare at her profile. Um. Oh. Well, there was an aspect of my perfect plan I hadn't accounted for.

My bedroom window was too high up to reach from the outside. I rolled my shoulders. "I'll figure something out when the time comes."

Just as we pulled onto the road, headlights appeared behind us. We both screeched, then Meryl rammed her foot into it and we barreled around the S-curve way too fast.

I white-knuckled the dashboard. "Be careful!"

"I'm trying!" We screeched around a few more curves, Meryl's tires going off the side of the pavement more than once. She fought to bring her fishtailing car under control. "I need to pull off and let them pass us. My car doesn't have enough power. Watch for a spot."

My eyes tracked the dark edge of the road until we passed a U-shaped turnout I knew to be the Bear Tracks picnic area. "Turn here," I hollered, "and cut the lights!"

Meryl did so, deftly skidding in behind a stand of Ponderosa pine and dousing the headlights simultaneously. The move would've impressed Austin Powers himself.

We unhooked our seatbelts simultaneously and slid down in our seats, but Meryl kept her head up enough to watch Luke and his date drive by. I saw the lights flash in our windows, then Meryl exhaled with gusto. "Good. They're oblivious."

"There's a shocker."

We watched Luke's taillights disappear into the distance, then we sat in the idling, blacked-out car and exchanged a "PHEW!" glance. Nerves made us snicker, then giggle, and finally bust into huge belly laughs. It helped us release the adrenaline built up in our systems.

"Come on. Let's go," I said, wiping tears from my eyes. I unfolded myself from the seat and checked my appearance in the visor mirror. YIKES! Low-crawling is NOT fashion-forward, I assure you. "God, I'm covered in foliage."

"Well, at least you didn't get caught."

"Good point!" I was instantly cheered.

Meryl pulled out of the picnic area and headed toward Caressa's at a much safer clip, while I picked twigs and dirt out of my hair and clothing. By the time we arrived in Caressa's portico, I was just about back to normal.

Caressa was waiting for us, and she pulled open the passenger door and grinned. "How did it go?"

I sniffed. "Piece of cake."

"What?" Meryl groaned. "Sometimes, Lila, I just want to kill you."

I stepped from the car exuding exaggerated über-coolness. "Well, kill me later. We have a dumb supper to attend."

It didn't take us very long to get all the food ready and lined up on the counter. When we'd finished, Meryl did the whole sage-stick purification routine, then gathered us in Caressa's bedroom to go over last-minute details. We still had to write out our prayer/wishes. I sprawled on Caressa's bed, sort of tuning out Meryl, and started thinking about my mom. A part of me felt guilty because, to be honest, I don't think about her that much these days. She died eons ago, when I was a preschooler, from breast cancer.

I hate to admit it, but I barely remember her anymore. I used to be able to close my eyes and smell her perfume or hear her voice, but not for the past few years. Sometimes I have to work really hard just to envision her face without referring to a photograph as a reminder.

The whole dead-relative-coming-to-supper aspect of

this thing kinda gave me the yeeks at first, but after I thought about it, I liked the idea that my mom's spirit would be in on the whole who-should-Lila-date deal.

"Lila, did you hear me?"

I jumped, blinking up at Meryl. "Huh?"

She sighed. "I swear, if you screw this up—"

"I won't, I won't. Promise." I didn't tell her I'd been thinking about Mom, because I know Meryl and she would've felt guilty for threatening me while I'd been reminiscing. Meryl is supersensitive about hurting people, which is one of her nicest qualities. "What were you saying?"

"I was reminding you guys that no one can speak after midnight, especially in the feast room."

We nodded.

"Okay, then. We're almost set." Meryl held out her palm. "Do you have gel pens?"

I leaned to the side and pulled three white pens from the back pocket of my Lucky Brand jeans. "And I got some black notecards, too. Somewhere." I patted my pockets again, coming up empty, and my heart dropped. "Uh-oh."

"You gave them to me, remember? They're right

here." Caressa snatched them up off her nightstand and passed one to each of us. She clutched hers to her chest and sort of shivered. "This is the exciting part."

"Excellent," Meryl said. "Let's write them out. And don't forget to—"

"Set them where our plates will go. We remember, Mom."

Meryl smirked at me, then bent over her notecard and started scribbling away, but I stared up at the ceiling for a moment, the end of the pen in my mouth. I didn't understand how Meryl could be so confident about this while I felt so intimidated. My future could very well depend on how I worded this little note to the cosmos. The pressure to get it exactly right was tremendous.

I mean, what if I asked for abundance, and the cosmos thought I was talking about my butt size? Or if I asked for a really *nice* guy and some Poindexter showed up, professing his undying geek love for me? Don't get me wrong, some of the guys in the computer crew at school are smokin' hot, and everybody knows they'll go way farther in life than most of the jocks. And then there was the whole Clay Aiken argument, if he was, in fact, straight, as I chose to believe. But still. Pocket protectors might be an indicator of future success, but in high school, they just aren't sexy.

After a moment, Meryl glanced up. "Having trouble?"

I cringed and nodded at the same time. "I'm afraid to screw it up. What'd you write?"

She glanced down at her card. "I pray/wish for a smart, cute guy who sees me for who I am and likes me because of it."

"Nice." I looked at Caressa. "Yours?"

"I pray/wish for a guy who doesn't think music is everything, and who likes me for ME and not for who my dad is."

"Okay, I see what you're both getting at." I took hold of my black notecard and sucked in a deep breath. After releasing it slowly through my nostrils, I wrote: *I pray/wish for a hottie rebel of a guy. One who breaks the typical guy mold and isn't anything like my train wreck of a brother, Luke. And make sure he likes ME rather than seeing me as a shortcut onto the police force.* I grinned up at my friends. "Done."

"Read it!" Meryl said.

I did.

Caressa laughed. "I'm SURE your dad would approve of a hottie rebel, Lila," she said sarcastically.

"Why do you think I prayed for that? What fun would a guy be if my dad DID approve of him?"

Meryl and Caressa and I shared a group hug for good luck, then we all headed confidently down the stairs, all jittery and giggly with excitement.

The feast room had been prepared. Our prayer/wish cards were in their designated spots. The time had come.

We huddled in the archway to the kitchen staring at the clock. Nobody drew a breath or uttered a word as the final fifteen seconds ticked away to midnight, but when the big hand and the little hand met up at the twelve, Meryl nodded to us, and the dumb supper commenced.

Meryl and Caressa worked like synchronized swimmers carrying the tablecloth, settings, and everything else into the candlelit feast room. I returned to the kitchen and lined up the food in proper order. I passed Meryl and Caressa each dish as it came time for them to carry it in to the table.

Everything was going so well. TOO well. I should've

known, the way my life had been swirling down the toilet lately, that it was too good to be true, but I was blinded by the ceremony and our reverent silence.

The nightmare happened between delivering the Cup-a-Soup course and the appetizer course. That's right, I didn't even get a chance to eat the feast laid out for us before it all got screwed up. Here's what happened: I had nuked the soup and placed the Styrofoam containers safely on a tray so Meryl and Caressa wouldn't spill them. They'd just trooped off with them, and I was taking the taquitos out of the oven when all of a sudden—

BAM, BAM, BAM!

It sounded like someone wanted to knock the freakin' door down. I jumped out of my skin and barely refrained from screaming. The no-talking rule had been hammered into my brain so solidly, though, I managed to stifle the noise against my fist. I set the cookie sheet of taquitos on the stove top with a clatter, sort of looking around frantically for Caressa. What should I do? It was her house, after all.

I couldn't answer it, could I?

That would mean talking, and—

The pounding sounded again, so I hurried toward the door to open it. I didn't want the supper to be ruined for Caressa and Meryl, too. With any luck, I could get rid of whoever it was before either of them noticed.

My hands shook as I worked the deadbolts, but I managed to unlock the door and yank it open before a new bout of knocking further destroyed our carefully cultivated silence. I just never expected to see Dylan Sebring on the other side.

Dylan Sebring?!?!?

Let me tell you a few things about Dylan. The first thing any human female with eyes would notice about the guy is his utter droolworthiness. No denying, Dylan had IT. The looks (vaguely Brad Pitt-esque), the bod (tight), the charm (dimples and all). All the girls in school wanted Dylan, as evidenced by the high-pitched titters that abounded whenever he walked through the halls. All the girls except MOI, of course, because Dylan Sebring, hottieness notwithstanding, had several strikes against him in the Lila book:

Strike One—Dylan is the lieutenant of the junior narc squad, aka the Police Explorers. GAG. Way too Luke-like.

Strike Two—He's also the captain of the WPHS ski team. Ho-hum, jocks. I mean, they look sexy and all in their tight uniforms, but jocks are total Cheerleader Food, and I refuse to eat from a communal trough, so to speak.

Strike Three—Dylan is mondo POPULAR; in other words, wayyyyyyyyyy out of my league.

Strike Four—(even though you only need three for an OUT)—Dylan knows all this.

He is SO not my kind of guy. Give me a rocker with long hair, frequent visits to detention, and a pierced lip any day. I mean, my dad totally APPROVES of Dylan. No thanks.

Still, his drool factor momentarily tripped me up.

"Uh . . . hi," I sort of rasped, casting a quick peek over my shoulder. I didn't want the entire dumb supper to be ruined by his intrusion, nor did I really want him to know what we were up to. When Dylan's little cop radio crackled with voices, I pushed him out into the portico and pulled the door shut behind us. "Turn that thing down!"

"Gee, sorry." He twisted a little knob on the contraption, lowering the volume.

"Why were you knocking so hard?" I asked, breaking the no-talking rule fully and no doubt destroying my chances at true love forever—big surprise. "Do you know what time it is?"

"I do." He smiled. "Apparently you don't, though."

My stomach tightened. "What are you talking about?"

Dylan crossed his arms and a muscle in his jaw jumped in a way that was both sexy and annoyingly coplike. Those two things should NOT go together! "I'm talking about the fact that you're apparently grounded, and yet you aren't home."

I jutted out my chin, embarrassed and defensive both. "What's it to you?"

"It's nothing to me, but your dad is pretty pissed off."

GLUG. My heart dropped into my stomach. I don't know why, but I hadn't expected that. "M-my dad?"

"Yup. He couldn't break away, so he sent me over to pick you up and take you home." He grimaced, and for a moment I could almost believe that he felt sorry for me. Then I remembered . . . oh, yeah, this is DYLAN SEBRING. Mr. Play-by-the-Rules, suck up to my dad, big-brother clone. Riiiiiight. "I think you're way busted," he added unnecessarily.

I stepped back, partially because I couldn't believe my dad had found me out, and partially because I was so mortified by this blatant display of parental disregard for my reputation. HOW HUMILIATING for Dylan to know just exactly how short a leash my father kept me on. "I don't have to go with you."

"He thought you'd say that." Dylan fished in the front pocket of his ugly blue Explorer uniform shirt. He came up with a folded piece of paper and extended it toward me. "This is from your dad."

I unfolded it and recognized the handwriting right off. Judging by how hard he had pressed the pen into the paper—not to mention the message itself—I was in deep doo-doo: *Lila Jane Moreno, get your butt home and don't you move a muscle until I get there. If you give Lt. Sebring*—Lt. Sebring . . . SCOFF!—*any trouble, I'll hear about it. This is the last straw.*

Gulp. Double gulp.

Just then, Caressa and Meryl cracked open the front door and peered out. Neither of them spoke. I turned toward them, trying to keep the fear out of my expression.

"I'm sorry, guys. My dad busted me. I have to go with *him*"—I jerked my thumb over my shoulder at Dylan—"but just go on and finish without me."

"What are you guys doing?" Dylan asked.

"Studying," I snapped, as I took my coat from Meryl, who'd quickly retrieved it from where I'd hung it over the banister inside, "as if it's any of your business."

"Yeesh, don't shoot the messenger. I just asked a simple question," Dylan said, just as Meryl exclaimed, "Lila!"

"What?" I spread my arms and glared at her. Granted, I wouldn't usually be this snarky, not even to Dylan, but I had to save face! I was embarrassed, not to mention angry that our dumb supper plans were ruined. "It doesn't matter. He's just an extension of my dad's posse anyway."

Meryl balked, then gave a strained smile to Dylan. "Don't mind Lila. She doesn't know what she's saying. She hit her head earlier on my windshield."

"Stop talking," I told her, with some sense of urgency. "You're not supposed to talk!"

"Forget it." Meryl shrugged, looking flustered and defeated all at once. "We can't finish without you anyway. It wouldn't be the same."

"Wow." Dylan sort of jostled me in the shoulder with his elbow. "I didn't know you were such a brainiac. You make them study in silence, and they won't even finish without you?"

ARGH!!!!!

"Just . . . let's go." I flounced past him, calling back over my shoulder to my friends, "I'll email you guys!"

He followed me, completely oblivious to my evil mood. "So, do you tutor people other than your friends?"

"I don't tutor anyone, Sebring!"

He just laughed, which torqued me off. "Oh, sure. So I don't fit your profile of a potential student. I see the writing on the wall."

I spun back toward him, poking my finger toward his chest for emphasis. "Let's get one thing straight. You don't know me, you aren't a part of my universe, and I'm not going to discuss my life with you. Do my father's bidding, like the narc you are, but STOP TALKING TO ME BECAUSE I'M NOT INTERESTED IN CONVERSATION."

Okay, harsh. But, it truly was my humiliation talking.

Dylan's eyes narrowed briefly, then he held up his

palms as if to say, "have it your way," and headed past me to the car. I beat him there and yanked my door open before he tried to be gentlemanly and do it for me. I was already feeling a bit ashamed that I'd taken my annoyance out on him. Then again, HE ruined my night!

I yanked the seatbelt across my body, then pretended not to watch Dylan walk as he rounded the hood of his car and angled himself into the driver's seat, but I will admit, it was hard. He made my heart pound, which sorta pissed me off because I didn't WANT him to make my heart pound. I wanted him to go away. Far, far away.

For a few, blissful moments, he drove in silence, but the guy just couldn't keep his mouth shut.

"Nice night, isn't it?"

Fuming silence.

"So, why didn't you go to homecoming?"

Low blow. Was the question as innocent as it sounded, or was he trying to point out that I was dateless? Girls quite regularly said one thing and meant another, but whoever knew with guys? Either way, it just wasn't an appropriate question. It's like asking a girl how much she weighs or what size her jeans are! "Bite me, Sebring," I said, in this singsongy tone.

He laughed, soft and low, a sound that made my skin tingle. "Not unless you ask real nicely, Moreno," he teased.

EEEK! I focused on the trees flanking the road out my side window, with my body squished as far away from Dylan as I could get without actually cramming myself into the crack between the seat and the door. My night was ruined, my reputation besmirched. Now Dylan Sebring was saying things that sounded vaguely flirtatious, which *couldn't* be true.

God. I had to get out of the car and away from this guy who was so hot, but SO annoying and confusing at the same time.

four
* * * * * * * *
meryl

Gosh, what a terrible and abrupt ending to a night that
had started out so filled with hope. After Lila left with
Dylan Sebring (who is so very cute and looks really hot
in his uniform, despite what Lila says—and WHY was
she being so snotty to him?!), Caressa and I just felt icky
about the whole night. We couldn't very well start over
with the dumb supper. For one thing, it was past midnight, and we'd already broken the silence. And we
couldn't, in good conscience, have Lila's mother here as
a spirit guest when Lila herself was absent.

Now, I've discussed metaphysical ceremonies at
length with Reese and Kelly, the co-owners of Inner
Power where I work, and I know it's all about one's
intent rather than rules and regs. Regardless, it didn't

feel complete without Lila there. I don't know how to explain it. The three of us are the best of friends, without any of the favoritism that so often causes problems with groups of three friends. But Lila, she's like the spark that ignites our little triad. Caressa and I are perfectly comfortable in our own skin, but I think both of us secretly wish we were a little more like wild Lila.

So, it was all three of us for the supper or nothing.

Plus, Caressa and I were both preoccupied with worry that Lila would be grounded for life! How could we possibly focus on finding boys to date when she was going to be in so much trouble? We should've seen it coming. Well, in truth, we HAD seen it coming, but when Lila Moreno gets an idea in her mind, there is no deterring her. It's definitely one of her charms, but if she doesn't rein it in, it could also be her downfall.

I sat on the bottom step of the sweeping marble staircase in Caressa's entryway and laid the side of my face on the polished wood banister. My stomach felt tight and jittery. "That was purely awful."

Caressa nodded, sliding down the wall to sit on the floor. She hugged her long legs to her chest and rested her chin on her knees, then blew out a big sigh. "Mer, I knew Lila was pushing her luck with this latest scheme. If I did half the things she did, my parents would kill me. She's going to give me gray hair before I'm twenty."

"Yeah. But that's one of the things I like about Lila the most. She jumps in with both feet." Without looking first!

"True. I just wish—" She pressed her lips together.

"What?" I asked Caressa. Her eyes looked sad.

"Eh, nothing. I just wish we'd finished."

I knew Caressa was really let down about the whole dateless thing. She wanted to know who her prospects were. Well, we all did. But Caressa had an extra strike against her that Lila and I didn't. She's GORGEOUS. Her mom's Hawaiian and her dad's African American, and let me tell you, she got the very best of both of their genes. She has this amazing, smooth, caramel-colored skin, as though she's always kissed by the sun; long wavy brown hair naturally highlighted with deep copper; and vivid green, slightly tilted eyes. Plus she's supersweet.

Don't misunderstand me, I think Lila and I are both cute enough girls (though I could do without my red hair and pale skin), but Caressa's in a whole other league. Lucky her, right? Not really. Lila and I aren't sub-jected to much cattiness from the other girls, because they don't see us as competition. Poor Caressa intimi-dates both the boys *and* the girls, but the girls really take it out on her. If only they could step back and see how truly vulnerable, humble, and genuine she is . . .

But, anyway.

The whole dumb supper debacle was depressing, and I didn't want to dwell on everything that could've been. Instead, I stood. "Well, let's clean up. I just have a creepy feeling now and I kind of want to go home. I hope that's okay."

"You go ahead, Mer." Caressa smiled sadly at me. "I'll clean up. It'll give me something to do since you won't be spending the night after all."

I have to say, I was glad she offered. Something told me I should go home right then. I felt compelled. "Are you sure?"

"Uh-huh. Go on. I like cleaning. It calms me."

"Okay, then." She stood as I put on my coat, then hugged me good-bye. I squeezed back.

"Drive carefully."

"I always do."

Caressa raised one of her perfect eyebrows in a skeptical expression and planted her fists on her hips. "That's not what Lila told me about the drive over here earlier tonight."

I giggled. "Yeah, yeah. 'Night, Caressa." And with that, I jogged across the portico and got into my trusty Volvo.

The drive from Caressa's to my house is always pitch black. There aren't streetlights up here in the mountains unless you are on the main roads. I mean, I had my headlights, but driving home always felt like being inside a fragile bubble of light that could pop at any moment and leave you choking on pure, unending blackness. That lovely thought made me shiver, so I turned up my radio for company. I was cheered to hear they were playing Beethoven's "Triple" Concerto in C Major, Op. 56. It has always been one of my favorites.

I usually choose to listen to the classical station from Vail, because the music is beautiful and uplifting. I know people think I'm strange because I don't listen to the regular music most kids do. Really, if I wanted to switch to the pop station, all I had to do was press a button. My parents weren't there to admonish me, and it wasn't as if I've never heard pop music. When I spend time with Lila and Caressa, I listen to what they want to hear. But they're also respectful of my family's way of life and open to new experiences, so sometimes we listen to classical. That's what I love about my best friends. They don't try to make me into someone I'm not, even though I must seem like a space alien to them at times, and they try to show enthusiasm for my interests, too.

The whole point is this: my parents might have raised us in a nontraditional way, but I don't mind it. In fact, I like it for so many reasons. My parents never seem as harried and stressed out as other adults, and our house is always a haven.

Sure, I used to feel left out when I was little and all my friends were watching cartoons that were off-limits to me, but I got over it. Now I don't even have the urge to watch television. No. Really. I don't.

I don't judge other people for how they choose to spend their free time, but the whole television thing seems like an egregious waste of time to me.

That's just me. Life is a choice.

I swear, though, sometimes I feel like my peers' heads are so full of this television show or that movie, this new hot star or that reality show (a concept I can't quite grasp, even though Lila has tried to explain it to me on more than one occasion), that they forget to just sit back and think about things. Life, themselves, world events, the future, the universe, goals. I know I'm eccentric, but I like being different, and I like thinking about all these subjects and more.

So, anyway, I was driving down Meadow Brook Road, watching carefully for deer or elk on the road and doing exactly that—thinking about stuff—when all of a sudden I heard this big *POW*, and my car screeched and swerved a little. A surge of adrenaline pushed my heart into my throat, and I steered the car over to the rocky shoulder. I could hear the flap-flap-flapping as I drew to a stop, and there was no mistaking the unusual lopsidedness to my car. Damn, a flat.

I'd never had a flat before. Why now?

My palms started to sweat and tears stung my eyes. It wasn't because I was afraid of changing a tire, per se. I just wasn't too thrilled to have to change my tire on a pitch black mountain road, alone, in the middle of the night. Naturally, I heard an animal howl off in the distance, because it was just the perfect thing to feed my fears. Right at that moment, I wished like crazy that my parents believed in cell phones.

I knew the tire wasn't going to change itself, but I still couldn't bring myself to get out of the car. What a chicken! I had been born and raised in the mountains, and I usually liked the silence and the darkness. *Usually.* The inky sky made a much better backdrop for the stars than the light-polluted city sky down in Denver. But the same inky sky felt foreboding as I sat there with a flat tire and a fast heartbeat.

Trying to steady myself and squelch my fears, I glanced up into the sky and tried to convince myself of how much I loved the darkness. I took a deep breath and picked out some of my favorite constellations. Ursa Major was easy to find. Always is. I think of it as the layman's constellation, because even though it's the third largest, it's mainly known as the home of the Big Dipper, which makes me feel kind of sad for it. All that vastness and really only one claim to fame.

I was happy to see Orion, master of the winter skies, already, considering it was only late September. I've always liked the mythological story behind Orion and the picture it puts in my head. Orion is said to lord over the heavens from late fall to early spring, with his hunting dog, Sirius, trailing at his feet.

How cute. I love dogs.

I smiled as I picked out the three stars which form Orion's belt: Mintaka, Alnilam, and Alnitak. As always, I felt awed by their presence. I just think it's amazing that even the Bible makes reference to these stars, and yet here they are, steadfast in the twenty-first century. That constancy over thousands of years makes me realize what a minuscule part of the universe my little life is.

Stargazing was making me feel better, though I still had a flat to deal with. I knew I'd deal with it better if I was calm, so I kept my eyes aimed upward. Tonight was the transit date of the principal star of Andromeda, so I searched for and found it as well. That was a mistake, though, because it made me think of the story behind it, which made me think of Lila getting busted, which got me all upset and worried once again.

See, Andromeda was the daughter of Cepheus and Cassiopeia, and Cassiopeia was totally vain. Even more vain than Lila's brother's girlfriend, Miffany, if you can believe it. Get this: Cassiopeia believed she and Andromeda were more beautiful than any of Poseidon's many nymphs, and she taunted the God of the Seas until he just couldn't deal. (What kind of dummy would be so shortsighted as to taunt the God of the Seas?) Infuriated, Poseidon punished Cassiopeia by tying her daughter to a rock. Naked. Yep, naked. And, he left poor, naked Andromeda there to be sacrificed to some dreadful sea monster.

Can you say harsh?

I know it's a stretch, but I couldn't help but think of Lila and how totally in for it she was with this last stunt. She'd taunted her dad with disobedience just like Cassiopeia had taunted the God of the Seas. I sure hoped Chief Moreno didn't pull a Poseidon on her and tie her naked to the proverbial rock as punishment. Enough of that. Worry never made the future better, it just stole energy from the present.

Unfortunately, the *present* included me, a desolate mountain road, and a flat tire. Swell.

Just as I was getting ready to suck it up and deal with the dilemma, two headlights blazed through my back window into my rearview mirror and blinded me. For a split second, I felt relieved . . . but then I got scared. We all hear stories about creepy guys who victimize stranded motorists, and I was spooked to begin with. I quickly locked all my doors, slipped my car into drive, then sat there with my foot on the brake pedal but ready to move to the gas pedal just in case I needed to make a squealing getaway. If anyone scary approached the car, I was GONE, flat tire or not.

I kept my eyes glued on the side mirror, trying to ignore the OBJECTS IN MIRROR ARE CLOSER THAN THEY APPEAR warning, which was hard. First, I saw a silhouette of a person getting out of the car and heading toward me. I didn't move, don't even think I drew a single breath. But I lucked out! When he finally got close enough for me to see his features, I recognized the guy approaching as a fellow student from school.

It was That Bosnian Guy. Isn't that awful? I didn't even know his name, because everyone at school referred to him as That Bosnian Guy. All we knew was, he and his family came here as refugees (a word with an undeserved negative connotation), and now he was attending WPHS.

I've never paid him much attention, but I was SO relieved to see him. At least I didn't feel like I'd be ax-murdered in my car. I put the car in park, engaged the emergency brake, then rolled down my window a crack. "Hi."

"Hi." He smiled and ran one hand through his golden blond hair, from front to back. The motion made my throat dry, for some strange reason. "Do you need some help?"

I twisted my mouth to the side. "I have a flat tire." I probably didn't have to demonstrate my keen grasp of the obvious with that statement, what with my car dipping to one side and my rear tire completely devoid of air, but I felt all fluttery-nervous around him. The words had just come out in a blurt.

"I will change it for you if you like," he said. He speaks perfect English, but he has this yummy accent that makes even a mundane statement sound exotic.

"I'd be really grateful if you'd help me with it."

"No problem." He shrugged out of his ski parka and laid it on the roof of my Volvo. "Unpop the trunk, please."

I bit my lip to hold back the smile, then UNpopped the trunk as he asked. I have to say, he looked GREAT with that T-shirt stretched across his chest. He wasn't a musclebound guy. More tall and lanky, with long, lean muscles. But he looked fantastic in jeans and a T-shirt. "You go to WPHS, right?" I asked, just so he'd know I recognized him.

He nodded. "I am Ismet."

"Nice to meet you. I'm Meryl."

"Meryl"—he said my name in that REALLY cute accent, and it made my tummy swirl in the most delicious way—"yes. I think I have seen you in the halls. Are you in grade eleven?"

"Yes."

"I am, too. Your father, he is a teacher, yes?"

"And the football coach," I said, rolling my eyes. "And also the school disciplinarian."

He pulled this fake scared face that was so adorable. "I am lucky to have never met him, then."

I laughed at that, finally feeling safe, but his comment made me think. Wasn't it just an example of how virtually ALL the guys who knew my dad felt? No wonder I've never had a date.

He pointed to my tire then and got down to business. "If you want to come out of the car, I will change it. I would lift the car with you inside, but it is not so safe."

I must've looked uncertain, even though I felt fine, because he hiked his thumb over his shoulder, indicating his car. "My sister, Shefka, is here with me if that makes you feel better. I will bring her up with me."

I didn't want him to think I was some skittish, ethnocentric American who was afraid of foreigners, so I said, "Oh, it's okay. I'm not afraid of you. I was just . . . sort of afraid in general, to have a flat on this dark road, this late at night. I've been sitting here for who knows how long, just trying to get up the courage to get out of the car."

"Ah. I can understand. I was not too confident to approach your car, either," he joked.

Is that not so sweet? Most guys act so annoyingly macho, and he was the antithesis of that. For him to admit that he wasn't immune to the heebie-jeebies made me like him even more.

I got out of the car and met him around back, where he was rooting around in the trunk. He fished out a flashlight and handed it to me. I turned it on, said a silent prayer of thanksgiving that the batteries were fresh, and then held it over the trunk to help him see better.

"It is late," he said, just making small talk while he

got out the jack and spare. "Did you go to the home-coming?"

HOW EMBARRASSING. I actually looked away from him when I shook my head no, but then he said, "I did not go either," and I felt instantly better.

"What are you doing out so late?" I asked, though it was none of my business.

"My sister and I, we visit friends from where I used to live—"

"Bosnia?"

He smiled. "Yes. They live in Idaho Springs now." He shrugged. "We were watching DVDs."

I nodded, not really sure what to say next. I could ask him what DVDs they'd been watching, but I wouldn't recognize any of the titles anyway, and the conversation would fizzle. I decided, instead, to focus on the tire. It looked more than flat, it looked shredded. "I can't believe the tire did that."

"It looks bad. You are a good driver to keep the car on the road after such a blowup." He smiled again.

I smiled back, because he'd called it a *blowup* instead of a *blowout*, which was supercute. "Thank you. My dad would be happy to hear that."

We both laughed, and then he got to work on the flat.

I know it was probably the typical, unfeminist girl thing to do—say yes to the GUY changing the tire for me—but hey. It was, as I've said, the middle of the night, pitch dark, and I've never changed a tire except for practicing with my dad. But that had been in a heated garage with fluorescent lights, and he talked me through every step.

Things got more comfortable between Ismet and me after that. I held the flashlight, and we chatted about school while he worked. Eventually his sister, Shefka, came up and hung out while Ismet finished. Shefka is a freshman, but she seems very smart and mature for her age. She was friendly.

Ismet had removed the shredded tire and he was lifting the spare into place just as I glanced down at him. The muscles of his back flexed with his effort and my awareness of him just sort of prickled up my spine. The realization struck me like a lightning bolt: *HEY, THIS GUY'S REALLY DATEABLE CUTE, in an exotic, foreign sort of way.*

Exotic and foreign were good things!

Just like that, with one split second of fresh insight, I started looking at Ismet in a completely different light. I mean, it never crossed my mind to think of That Bosnian Guy as a dating prospect, and now I couldn't think of him in any other way. He'd sort of fallen into my life at the precise moment when I needed help, just MOMENTS after I'd left the dumb supper, and—

Wait a minute. The dumb supper!

Shock riddled through me.

Ismet was the first guy I'd seen, and there was all this unexpected but interesting electricity between us. Could it be that Lila's, Caressa's, and my intent with the dumb supper was strong enough to have set things in motion, even without finishing the ceremony?

I blinked down at him, and my heart did this exhilarating pitter-pat. Why hadn't I ever noticed how adorable he was before??? I recalled how compelled I'd felt to leave Caressa's, even though my parents thought I'd be spending the night there. Why WAS that? Fate? The same fate, perhaps, that brought Ismet and Shefka down Meadow Brook Road *exactly* when I needed them?

Excitement zinged through me, obliterating all the

bad feelings I'd had earlier. I bit my bottom lip and hugged one arm around my torso to hold back the shivers.

This was it! Destiny had come knocking.

I couldn't wait to get home to email Lila and Caressa!

five

caressa

After my girls were gone, the house didn't look all fes-
tive and mysterious to me anymore, like it had when we
still nursed hope that the dumb supper would give us
some much-needed insight. It just looked like a mess,
and it felt really empty with Mom and Dad gone for the
night, too. I couldn't face cleaning up the feast room yet.
UGH! Seeing all the decorations, candles, and food
would only bum me out even more than I already was.

Instead of doing what needed to be done, I headed
up to my bathroom for a stress-relieving minispa treatment. They always help me think and get my head
straight. I'd received shipments from both Sephora.com
and blissworld.com this week, and I had yet to try out
any of my new products. Fun, fun, fun!

I switched into my favorite flannel pajamas, then started out with "the refining facial" scrub from La Mer, which I'd wanted to order for SO long, but I'd had to save up for it. (Expensive!) It actually has diamond dust and spun-smoothe quartz mixed in fermented sea muds and other kewl scrubby stuff. It made my skin feel absolutely amazing—a magic trick considering I was on the verge of my usual monthly period-induced breakout. My friends accuse me of having perfect skin, but they're so wrong. I get zits just like everyone else.

I dotted some Peter Thomas Roth AHA/BHA acne-clearing gel on the worst areas, then decided, in light of recent events, that I needed a special treat. I sneaked into my mom's bathroom and used a little bit of her Z. Bigatti Re-Storation cream, taking great care to put it back exactly where I'd found it. I was SO not allowed to use the stuff, because it cost something like five hundred bucks for eight measly ounces, but I needed the pick-me-up. Surely Mom would understand if she found out, not that she would.

It's not like she couldn't afford more.

I have to say, there are definitely cool benefits to having a rich dad. I would *never* flaunt money, but having access to it and being able to buy nice stuff is better than scrounging pennies to buy Noxzema. I'd be a liar if I claimed otherwise.

A lot of my friends still ride the bus, and I drive a BMW. That's not to say that my parents are totally indulgent. Believe me, I'm grateful for every luxury I have. I mean, I still shop at Target and stuff. But it is nice knowing I can shop at Saks or Barneys, too, if I want to.

Ah, but every coin has two sides. Having a famous dad puts me in a very awkward position. Not that guys my age show any interest in me, but if they ever DO, how will I know if they like ME or just think it's cool to go out with a Grammy-winning musician's daughter? Other than Lila and Meryl, I never know if people want to be friends with ME, or if they want a friend with so-called status (which is a bogus concept anyway).

Please. If they only knew, I live exactly the same life they do. My face breaks out, my parents bug me, I experience angst over whether these jeans make my butt look fat, or those sleeves give me wobbly STA (substitute teacher arms).

I'm NORMAL. Parents are PARENTS. Being a teenager is being a teenager—period.

I love my dad, but to me he's JUST Dad. Sure, I love listening to his music and I'm proud of him for all he's accomplished in his life, but no more proud than Lila is of her dad (well . . .) or Meryl of hers. I just wish more people would understand that, but then again, I don't need a huge circle of friends. I'm good with Lila and Meryl.

Slightly cheered by the way my face looked and felt, I decided to treat my hair, too. I applied some Moltobene Clay Esthe pack and then sucked it up and went downstairs to tackle the cleanup while the treatment worked its wonders on my locks.

It was weird, though. Just entering the feast room, which was really just our breakfast room all decked out, made me walk more softly and try to be mondo churchlike quiet. I glanced around at ALL the food we didn't get to eat, then took a fork to the Sara Lee cheesecake. It, of all things, I did not want to waste. I sat there eating, wondering WHY things had to go wrong before any of us got the chance for our wishes to come true, and then it hit me. Why couldn't I just go ahead and bless the ceremony, light the candles, and burn our prayer/wish cards like we'd planned? It couldn't hurt, I figured. Either it worked or it didn't, but it wouldn't even have the chance to work if I didn't torch those cards. I just didn't feel right about throwing them in the trash.

I started out by leaving the room, then reentering it backward, like Meryl had told us to do. I walked over to the spirit chair, laid my hands on the back, and said a quick, silent prayer about Lila's mom. When I was done, I lit the white votive candle and placed it in front of her place setting.

From there, I moved from place to place, lighting the black votive candles and setting the little glass cups that held them just at the top of each of our plates. I sat down in my spot and took one bite of each food item. (Okay, I took a few extra bites of cheesecake, I admit it.) By then, the black votive candles were nice and melty, and I got down to business. I burned Lila's card first, because she really NEEDED something to go right in her life. I added a little prayer that her dad didn't hammer her too hard for sneaking out. Then I burned Meryl's, and last I burned mine. I felt exhilarated when they were all gone! I don't know if it made a difference, but it definitely gave me some closure on the whole screwed-up event.

I finally felt ready to clean up and move on.

Once I'd set the room back to order, I rinsed off my hair pack, dried my now luxuriously soft 'do, then carried my journal down to the living room. Whenever things are crazy for me, I spill my guts about whatever's going wrong in my journal. I get a new journal every Christmas, and each one has been like a best friend. I can be kind of shy, and writing down my thoughts never fails to make me feel better.

So, I'm sitting there in the red leather chair-and-a-half by the fireplace when all of a sudden, a CD falls off the shelf ACROSS THE ROOM and lands on the Aubusson rug. I half jumped out of my skin. I wasn't anywhere NEAR that shelf, I swear, and none of the CD cases had been hanging off even slightly.

Seriously wiggy. I mean, I'm sitting there writing in my journal about *how much I wanted our wishes to come true even though the supper failed,* and all of a sudden that particular CD comes shooting out of the shelves! Well, I guess it didn't actually SHOOT out if we're going to get technical, it just kinda fell. But still. There is no explanation for it. Our housekeeper just cleaned in there today, and she's sort of obsessive-compulsive about orderliness. She spends at least an hour making sure all the jewel cases line up. (I know, weird. But at least I don't have to do it.)

There wasn't an earthquake or a semi driving into the side of the house or anything, so why did the CD fall???

I was überwigged, feeling all Stephen Kingish about the house and stuff, but I scrambled out of the chair anyway and sort of approached the CD cautiously like it was a poltergeist or a bomb or a crazy person or something. My parents travel quite a bit, and I'm WAY okay with being home alone, but right then I was SO wishing I wasn't by myself. YUGGGS, I just managed to totally psych myself out about the whole thing. The hair on the back of my neck actually stood up on end!

Despite the fact I was so creeped, I picked up the CD and looked at the front, and I was SO shocked. GUESS WHOSE CD IT WAS??? This really ultra-sweatworthy young blues musician named Bobby Slade. I don't know if that means anything to anyone else, but to me it was like a big whack-a-mole bop on the head from the universe saying, "Wake up, Caressa!"

Bobby Slade is super wicked hot! He totally recorded

his first album at age SIXTEEN!!! He's a prodigy, according to my dad, and he's twenty-one now and really successful. There is this one photo of him in the liner notes of the CD—OHMIGOD, SWOON. He's wearing worn-out jeans, no shirt, no shoes, and holding his guitar all casual-like in front of his muscular chest. He has a tatt on his upper arm of some kind of Chinese symbol. It's just . . . wow.

Anyway, I put the CD away and didn't make the connection right away, but it finally hit me.

I burned the wish cards.

The supper worked!

I'm almost 100 percent sure that the universe was telling me Bobby Slade is the guy for me! I know what everyone will say when I tell them: CARESSA, YOU'RE NUTS! HE'S A FAMOUS PERSON! But, it all makes sense from my perspective. So many regular guys get all glazed over when they meet my dad, because he's famous. They want to touch his Grammy statues and hear about his touring days. Whatever. But, Bobby Slade wouldn't be all starstruck about my dad, because he's a star himself! He has his own freakin' Grammy statues!

Bobby Slade is exactly what I asked for in my

prayer/wish, even though I hadn't realized it until that CD took a digger. Maybe, all along, I needed to find a guy who could hold his own in the fame department in order for my dad's identity not to be an issue. Maybe THAT is what the dumb supper needed to tell me.

I started scribbling in my journal about Bobby, brainstorming different ways I could meet him in person. I'm still not sure about how to pull that off, but that's not what the dumb supper was supposed to help us figure out. It was supposed to point us toward WHO we might date, and it did that swimmingly. I can work out the rest on my own.

I could totally fall in love with Bobby Slade!!!

I think I already have!

I was so freakin' jazzed, I ran right upstairs to email Lila and Meryl.

Six

***   ***   ***   *

When I woke up early the next morning, the house was still dim and quiet, thank God. I should've been tired, but I was too amped up about my inevitable punishment. I was SO dreading facing my dad, and the stress stuck in my stomach like a congealed clump of elementary school mac and cheese. GLURG. I decided I should take advantage of this time to check in with Caressa and Meryl before the long arm of the law reached out to crush me. I had no idea if my dad would restrict me from the phone, the Internet, the television, or what, but it seemed likely. It also seemed really unfair. I mean, unless you're on *Survivor*, who can live without email access?!

But, I was absolutely dying to know what happened with the rest of the supperus interruptus, so I crept over to my computer and turned my sound volume off, then quickly signed on. Neither Caressa nor Meryl were on yet, but both of them had sent email messages in the middle of the night. Meryl's was first, and I couldn't wait to read it because she always had a calming effect on me. I double-clicked on it:

FROM: MerylM@Morgensternfamily.com
TO: LawBreakR@hipgirlnet.org, Lipstickgrrrrl@hip-girlnet.org
SUBJECT: The WEIRDEST thing!
TIME: 1:45:17 A.M., MST

Lila—

I hope everything's okay at home. I'm SO worried about you, and I'm SO sad that the dumb supper got messed up. I promise I won't say I told you so about getting busted, either. I just hope you're not grounded until after graduation. :-P Just so you know, we didn't keep going with the ceremony. We can try it again another solstice or equinox night, assuming you aren't on house arrest for the rest of your natural-born life. But, here's the real shocker: despite the problems, I think the purpose of the dumb supper might've worked!

I paused in reading Meryl's message to stave off a giant surge of nausea. Holy crap. Why hadn't I seen this coming? If even-keel, logical MERYL thought the dumb supper might've worked, I was full-on hosed. HELLO, had she forgotten that the first guy I'd come face to face with was DYLAN freakin'-totally-not-for-moi SEBRING?!?! My throat squeezed, probably with the effort of holding back a panic puke. Dylan Sebring wouldn't give me the time of day even if it was a direct order from my dad. Not to mention he had a GIRLFRIEND. This was ALL WRONG! Surely the dumb supper had to be OVER for the magic to happen, right? Dylan was NOT the rebel I wanted. He was a whole lot like my brother Luke . . . not to mention all my other brothers and my—horror of horrors—father.

If fate thought I was destined to be with a guy like DYLAN, then all I could say was, fate needed to back slooooowly away from the crack pipe.

With more than a little effort, I shook off my self-absorption and went back to Meryl's email. I scanned it quickly, reading about how she'd gotten a flat tire on the way home, *blah blah blah*, and the first guy she'd seen was That Bosnian Guy. She wrote:

His name is Ismet, in case you didn't know. Ismet Hadziahmetovic, and his sister's name is Shefka. Her name is pronounced pretty much how it looks, but his is pronounced ISH-met, not IZ-met or ISS-met.

You guys, he's SO sweet, and even though I've never really thought much about him before, he's very cute. But the point is, there he was, totally out of the blue with NO explanation for it except the dumb supper. I can't wait to hear what you both think about that.

L&K,

Meryl

I groaned, feeling truly ill, and fired off a quick response to Meryl:

FROM: LawBreakR@hipgirlnet.org

TO: MerylM@Morgensternfamily.com,

Lipstickgrrrrl@hipgirlnet.org

SUBJECT: re: The WEIRDEST thing!

TIME: 6:45:00 A.M., MST

Mer—

This is so cool about Ismet. I'm truly happy for you.

But please, please, PLEASE tell me that this could also be a coincidence and not a result of the dumb supper! :-O HELLO, two words for you: Dylan Sebring. ACKKKKKK! If the dinner DID work, fate is evil and my life rots. But we knew that.

Update: Dad's not up yet. I'm awaiting my sentencing. I feel all sick and nervous inside, sort of like Joan of Arc, waiting to be burned at the stake. (Or at least how I imagine she must've felt.) I'm afraid he's going to take away my computer! I mean, I can't think of a more heinous punishment, so what else? [FRET] Is that even legal anymore? Isn't Internet access a basic human right?

www.LilaLivesInHell.com

www.WishMeLuck.com

—Lila

Next, I double-clicked on Caressa's reply to Meryl, which she'd written hours ago. She hadn't even left her house, as far as I knew, so she couldn't have had a dumb supper epiphany. Surely she'd set Meryl straight about the Ismet coincidence.

Meryl!!!!

A hottie for Mer—that rocks, girl! I, too, had an interesting experience after you left, Lila. (HANG IN THERE! I'm sorry for what happened, too. You have to tell us what your dad does to you ASAP.) My cool thing seems directly connected to the dumb supper, too. I might not have believed it, but now that I read your tale, Meryl, it all makes TOTAL SENSE!!!

Here's what happened to me:

I was getting ready to clean up the rest of the feast room, when all of a sudden I decided, HEY, I might as well bless the supper and burn our prayer/wishes like we'd planned. Why not? I might be able to make things happen. Just call me *CHARMED*. [g] (Mer, it's a TV show reference, don't mind me.)

So, I placed my hands on the spirit chair, and closed my eyes. Lila, I really felt like your mom was there for us. I said a silent blessing for her and for the meal-that-never-was, then I went from seat to seat and lit the votive candles. The black ones were really mondo kewwwwwl!

I let them burn for a few minutes, and then I went from plate to plate and torched our prayer/wish cards. It was so fun and, like, empowering!

When I was done, I went into the living room to write in my journal about the whole thing. That's when the weirdness happened. I swear to you guys, I wasn't anywhere NEAR our CD shelves when *IT* happened . . .

It? IT?! I read on, faster and faster, until I got to the really out-there part. A GUY ON A CD?!? I SO could not believe that Caressa truly thought she was destined to fall in love with a (1) famous (2) twenty-one-year-old (3) blues musician (4) whom she had never met. Had she suffered some sort of mental break?

I stared at the screen for several moments, my jaw sort of hanging open with this totally unattractive mouth-breather expression. The world had definitely gone mad.

I didn't want to harsh on her mellow too badly, but I felt I needed to say something to Caressa about this little foray into psycholand. I clicked reply and typed:

FROM: LawBreakR@hipgirlnet.org

TO: MerylM@Morgensternfamily.com,
Lipstickgrrrrl@hipgirlnet.org

SUBJECT: re: The WEIRDEST thing!

TIME: 6:58:32 A.M., MST

Caressa—

I love you. You know I do. And, because of this, I feel I must point out a few things to you, for your own good:

1. Bobby Slade is TWENTY-ONE years old! HELLO!

2. Bobby Slade is a famous musician whom you have never met.

3. Bobby Slade is just a guy from a freakin' photo on some CD liner notes.

4. I'm no expert, but I don't think the dumb supper would include guys you saw in photos. DUDE, think about it. If that were the case, what if you'd seen someone creepily old, like the president of the United States on the front page of the paper, or something? YECCCH! Talk about grossity gross gross. Gross-o-rama. HORK! BUT . . . seeing some guy on a CD is sorta the same, even if Bobby S. is way cuter than the prez ever could be. It's still a huge-o stretch.

5. If none of my other arguments make you reconsider this, I must circle back to, BOBBY SLADE IS TWENTY-ONE YEARS OLD!!! That alone is enough to guarantee you guys probably aren't right for each other. I mean, come on. He's practically from another generation.

6. This last point is self-serving, but I do not WANT the dumb supper to have worked, because I had the sad misfortune of coming face to face with Dylan Sebring first. ACKKKKKK!!!!! I WOULD RATHER DIE A VIRGIN THAN HAVE SOME JOCKO COP WANNABE AS MY DESTINY!!!!!!!!!!!!!!

So, anyway, I think the CD must've been . . . I dunno, vibrations from the fridge or something that made it work its way out and you just happened to be there when it fell from the shelf. I DON'T KNOW! But, any other explanation is just too freaky woo woo to make sense.

I don't mean to poop in your punchbowl or anything, but we've got to keep a realistic perspective on this. You know I love you and Meryl both—like soul sisters. But, come on. Take Ismet . . . he's our age, he exists in our world, Meryl had actual contact with the guy, REAL conversation. Ismet, I can see.

Bobby Slade, though?

Girlfriend, crushing on Bobby can lead nowhere good. I hate to be the bad-news monger, but you worry me with this one. I only say this because you and Meryl are my BEST friends FOREVER.

There, I've said my piece. I'm off to prepare for my paternal smackdown. I hope you'll be thinking of me. I think I'm pretty well busted this time, so I'm trying to imagine the most heinous of punishments he can dole out. I have NO idea what I'm in for, but I'll keep you posted. See you at school.

—Lila, the damned

When I finally got the nerve up to creep downstairs to face the music, about an hour or so later, there was a note from my dad on the kitchen table:

Lila—
I had to go into the office early, but you're not off the hook. I will meet you here immediately after school. Don't be late, and I'm not kidding.
Love, Dad

I scoffed. What was with the LOVE, DAD ploy??? It sounded suspiciously like the grown-up version of the "this is going to hurt me more than it hurts you" pre-spanking spiel parents spouted, to guilt you into believing (1) the punishment was for your own good and (2) you deserved it. PLEASE.

But hey, at least I had a school day reprieve.

WPHS has this interesting way of scheduling classes. Each student takes six classes a semester (some seniors take five), but they each only meet every other day, for ninety-five minutes each, so we have more *immersion* in our subjects. We also have a sixty-five-minute period called "access," during which we can get extra help, or whatever, from our teachers. It's kind of cool only having three classes a day, but it's not all peaches and cream. If you *like* your classes, the day flies by. But, if you have a creep for a teacher or if you have no friends in class, it makes you yearn for the old, traditional fifty-minute period just to minimize the misery.

With my schedule, I had good days (aka classes with either Meryl or Caressa or both) and bad days (aka classes without anyone fun in them). Meryl was on the full advanced-placement track, whereas I only dabbled in AP (with science). Caressa, on the other hand, took a lot of creative electives in addition to the regular stuff, but we had a couple together.

Today, on one of the most stressful days of my high school career, it would only stand to reason that I had NO classes with either Meryl or Caressa. Who IS this Murphy guy, and why does he get to make up his own stupid laws?

We managed to converge at Meryl's locker for a few rushed minutes in the morning. The sounds of conversation, laughter, and slamming lockers eddied around us like we were three boulders stuck in the middle of a rushing stream. The halls were a-buzz with post-homecoming gossip, which hopefully meant Dylan hadn't had time to spread anything around about my so-called life. I checked a few faces but didn't see any indications that I was the official WPHS verbal whipping post of the day.

"So? What did your dad do?" Caressa whispered, clutching her books to her chest. Her eyes were round and concerned-looking. Meryl, meanwhile, was busy putting her textbooks into class-and-day order. I kid you not—Meryl is positively ANAL about school.

"He left me a note."

"Huh?" Meryl asked.

"He had to go to work early, so we didn't get to talk." I rolled my eyes, ever so slightly. "I have orders to meet him at home directly after school, though."

"Gosh." Caressa sighed. "I don't know. The anticipation seems worse than the punishment."

"You don't know what the punishment is yet," I countered.

"True. But, how bad can it be?"

I didn't want to contemplate it. "About the dumb supper," I started, hoping they'd both come to their senses in the light of day, "you guys don't really think it worked, do you?"

They exchanged a nervous glance, and my stomach sank.

"Look," Meryl said, in a tone I suppose was meant to console me, "the whole thing is about your intention. Maybe Caressa and I had stronger intentions, I don't know. I mean, I don't think you're stuck with Dylan Sebring if you don't want to be."

"Shhh! God, Mer!" I whipped a panicked glance at the faces around us. YEESH! I couldn't believe she'd just uttered that sentence aloud within the walls of WPHS. Dylan Sebring and I are not STUCK with each other. He has a *girlfriend,* for one thing. If anyone got wind of the notion that I thought he and I had something between us, I'd be more than just the verbal whipping post. I'd be the object of intense peer-group pity.

Did you hear about Lila Moreno crushing on Dylan Sebring? Pathetic, isn't it?

Ugh, ugh, ugh!

"Watch what you're saying," I rasped.

Meryl grimaced. "Sorry. I wasn't thinking."

I lowered my tone even more. "From now on, let's refer to him as . . ."

"How about Hutch? As in, Starsky and," suggested Caressa, sort of smiling.

"Hutch. That works."

"Who are Starsky and Hutch?" Meryl asked, looking baffled.

Caressa and I both started laughing, but then the bell rang. We said hasty good-byes and ran off toward our separate classes.

The day absolutely dragged, but I made it through relatively unscathed. I kept my ear perked for indications that any gossip about me had begun. By the end of the day, though, it became clear that my little problems weren't even a blip on the WPHS radar screen.

Dylan almost destroyed that bit of anonymity by having the nerve to smile and say hi to me in the hallway between my third class and access period. Please! Talk about a giant red flag. I ignored him, putting my head down and shouldering my way through the crowds. Despite my impending doom at the hand of my father, it was a relief for the school day to end. I felt like I'd spent a decade on death row, and today was my final dinner.

I arrived home twenty minutes after the last bell, like the obedient daughter I am (when I want to be). Dad's department vehicle was parked in the driveway, all somber and ominous-like. GLURK. Just like that, the nerves from the morning returned in a big rush. Deciding Caressa had been right, that it was better to KNOW my punishment than imagine it, I sucked it up and walked directly into the house.

Dad was sitting at the dining room table with the newspaper and a cup of coffee, the picture of paternal casualness. I shrugged off my backpack and dropped it on the floor, all the while eyeing him beneath my lashes.

He didn't look up, didn't say anything.

Bad sign number one.

Finally, he glanced up, then aimed his chin toward the chair at the far end of the table from where he sat. "Take a load off, Lila Jane."

Middle name. Bad sign number two.

I sat, slumped, then crossed my arms tightly over my torso. I wasn't trying to look defiant. It's just that my hands were shaking pretty badly, and I didn't want him to see the evidence of my fear. I decided to try and get this hell session off on the right foot. "I'm sorry about last night," I said, in a glum tone. Not as sorry as I was going to be in the next few minutes, probably.

Dad sighed, rubbing that worry line in between his brows. "I wish I could believe that."

"I am." Sorry I got busted, at least. I really didn't think I'd done anything so wrong.

Dad just nodded, studying me through narrowed eyes. His expression looked more sad than angry, which made my stomach hurt. It's one thing to piss your father off, but disappointing him feels a lot ickier. "I've thought a lot about your punishment, my dear daughter. Actually, about more than just that. I've thought about your behavior lately as a whole, and I've come to a few conclusions."

"Like what?"

"Like, you don't seem to respond too well when I restrict your actions or take away privileges."

My heart jumped and so did my hope. This sounded positive! "So, what then?"

"You need to learn discipline. And how to follow rules."

Did that mean he was going to enroll me in karate or something? My dad was a big fan of martial arts as an instructional tool on how to live life. Karate . . . how much would THAT rule? I decided to press for it. Heck, it was better than losing email privileges. "You're right. I do need that."

He nodded. "I want you to be involved in something that teaches you respect for yourself and others."

Karate. Definitely karate. I smiled. "Okay."

"Which is why you'll be joining the Police Explorers."

My brain shorted out, and for one long moment, I

sat there with a vacant stare and a frozen smile. "What about karate?"

My dad cocked his head to the side, looking utterly confused by my question. "Karate?"

Clearly, I'd misunderstood. Big, freakin' joke on Lila.

Suddenly, my father's despicable, unbelievable words lanced through my head like a machete, carving themselves onto the frontal lobe of my brain. Let me just say, in my WILDEST nightmares, I never would've imagined THIS punishment. The room seemed to tilt and roll, or maybe that was my stomach. I blinked convulsively at him, unable to wrap my brain around his words. Those awful words.

Had he ACTUALLY said I had to join the junior narc squad?!?!

KILL ME NOW!!

"W-wait a minute. What do you mean I have to join the narcs?" I asked, instantly numb with horror. I couldn't feel my hands, and my legs got so wobbly, I would've fallen had I not already been sitting.

"First of all, you need to stop referring to them as 'the narcs,' since you're going to be one of them. I don't want you to view this as a punishment really, Lila. Think of it as an opportunity for personal growth. It'll be good for you. I bet you'll even enjoy it," he said, all cheery and jovial-like. "It's a perfect and positive way for you to move away from some of your self-destructive behaviors."

Trust me, I wished I could self-destruct right there. To my horror, my eyes welled up with tears. "But, Dad—"

He dipped his chin and pierced me with a warning stare. "Lila, understand this is not up for discussion. I've made the decision. You will remain an active member of the Police Explorers until the end of the school year at least. In light of your blatant disobedience, this punishment is mild."

"Mild!?"

"Yes, mild. I could've taken your computer, your television privileges, your stereo—"

I shot to my feet and began crying in earnest. "You could take all that, shave my head, and send me to school buck naked. Even THAT wouldn't be worse than this!" I spread my arms wide. "Dad, I don't WANT to become a cop!"

"No one's saying you have to become a cop."

I didn't want to hear his excuses, and his calm tone

of voice made me want to flip out and have a meltdown like a toddler, lying on my back and kicking my legs around until I passed out. "You don't have a clue! I'm already a pariah in my school because YOU'RE a cop," I shrieked, threading my fingers into the front of my hair. "Not just a cop, but the *chief*! Can't you see that? You're destroying my life!"

He chuckled. He actually *chuckled*! "You certainly have a knack for overreacting, my dear daughter."

"I'm not overreacting! Can't you just send me to juvenile lockdown, or something? Sell me into slavery? Release me into the foster care system?"

That amused look stayed on his face, and he shook his head a little and sighed. "One day you'll thank me for this."

THANK him? The rant I wanted to spew was so virulent and overwhelming, I had to clamp a fist over my lips to keep it in. After a moment, I lowered my hand and asked, through a stuffy nose and clenched teeth, "I hope this counts as my community service, too."

"It does."

Thank God for small freakin' favors. "Are we done, then?"

"For the moment, yes." He checked his watch. "But you have about fifteen minutes to get ready."

"For what, now?" I wailed, my seriously boogery nose making my voice sound all thick and stupid.

"To go get fitted for your uniform. Lt. Sebring said he'd be glad to help you get what you need."

"Dylan?" I bug-eyed my dad. "Why HIM?"

"He's in charge of new recruits."

"I'm not a recruit! Recruit implies that someone talked you into WANTING to join. I'm doing this under extreme duress!"

Dad just ignored me. "Either way. I'm assigning you to work side by side with Lt. Sebring for the next several months. He'll show you the ropes and give me weekly reports on your cooperation and progress. Now, skedaddle." He winked. "We need to get you a uniform by next weekend."

I was afraid to ask. "Why?"

Dad looked at me like I was completely obtuse. "Well, so you can work the White Peaks football game, of course."

ACCCCCCCCKKKKKKKKKKKKKKKKKKKKK!

Not only was I a junior narc, but I was chained to

Dylan from now until next year, or until my brain exploded, whichever came first. AND, I had to wear that heinous uniform in front of The Whole School at the next football game.

It was BEYOND the worst punishment I could have ever imagined. It was a life-destroying punishment. I'd have to seek THERAPY when I was thirty, thanks to this cruelness.

My ears felt clogged and my nose was running. The torrent of tears had swelled my eyes into fat little sausage slits. And now, Dylan Freakin' Sebring would be at the front door in LESS than fifteen minutes. I spun on my heels, desperate to hit the makeup bag for some much-needed touch-ups, but my dad's words stopped me:

"One more thing."

What else? I thought. NOTHING he could tell me could be worse than the junior narc bomb he'd dropped. Feeling surly, I turned back to face him and cocked one eyebrow in question.

"You're still grounded."

"Shocker."

"*And* . . . no spending time outside of school with Meryl and Caressa for two weeks."

"Dad!"

"Their parents already know, so don't try your sneaking-out scam again."

Great, now I didn't even have a support system, and my two best friends' parents thought I was a hooligan. He might as well have killed me. No. On second thought, killing me would've been preferable to THIS.

It was official: My universe had come to a grinding, moaning halt . . . right on the proverbial railroad tracks.

Dear Lila—

I'm going to make your life an utter cesspool of misery, but someday you'll thank me for it.

Love, Dad

Riiiiiiight. And someday I'll thank my skin for zits, too.

Seven

·■·■■·■■·■

Let me tell you a few things I've learned in the past week and a half about men's double-knit, Dacron polyester cop pants:

(1) They feel like you have a garbage bag tangled around your legs. And they chafe. And they go swish, swish, swish between your thighs every time you take a freakin' step, almost as if you have the fattest legs in the universe.

(2) No matter how many different sizes they sell at that creepy cop uniform store, none of them fit you exactly right. Hence, they either make you look like (a) you're walking on a pair of overly plump, blue sausages (too small), or (b) you had an accident, and you're walking around with a giant pantload (too big).

(3) Anyone who wears these repulsive pants and isn't getting paid handsomely to do so is a major tool. (Apparently, myself included, even though I'm wearing them under duress.)

(4) They shouldn't give weapons to the people forced to don these freak-show pants, because wearing them makes you instantly suicidal (or homicidal).

I swear, if I ever find out who invented double-knit Dacron polyester and then thought, Hmm, this would make a GREAT pair of pants, I will hunt him down and kill him. I may revive him just to have the pleasure of killing him twice. And, yes, it HAD to be a HIM. No woman would invent fabric this WRONG.

The very WORST thing about these Satanic, beastly, vomitous pants we junior narcs are forced to wear is the fact that they actually make Dylan's butt look BETTER than it does naturally. On me, though, they have that unappealing my-butt's-so-huge-it-needs-its-own-zip-code effect. ARGH!!! Just when I thought life couldn't get any worse, I'm officially a junior narc AND I have a HUGE ROUND ASS. Perfect.

And that's JUST the result of the pants.

I have not even TOUCHED on the rest of this abhorrent

eunuch-form. But since I'm on a fairly decent rant, here goes:

(1) Ugly, western-style, light blue polyester shirt with fake buttons hiding a ZIPPER, for God's sake. It's on par with Velcro tennis shoes. I mean, really.

(2) Shiny, high-cut, Michelin Man parka, circa 1950, with a gigantic faux fur collar that would make an Eskimo cringe.

(3) Two-inch-wide, shiny, basketweave leather belt with a tacky "hi-ho!" pirate buckle.

The only good part of the uniform is the cool set of sh**kicker Rocky boots, but even THEY aren't cool enough to make up for the rest.

I. Wanted. To. Die.

Truly.

Not only was I a rookie narc with a Big Giant Polyester-encased Ass, but I had to wear that grotesque get-up in front of The Whole School. In less than thirty minutes, as a matter of fact. And I thought I had trouble getting dates two WEEKS ago. HA!

So there I sat in the briefing area we'd set up in one of the classrooms, a miserable fashion violator draped in double-knit and defeat. I was barely listening as

Dylan—whom I had to refer to as LIEUTENANT SEBRING when we worked (choke)—went over the evening's "strategy" with me and the rest of the narc squad.

Gimmeafreakinbreak—strategy?

Everyone acted like we were pulling top-level security duty for the First Lady, or for Brad and Jennifer—important people like that. COME ON, it was a stupid football game! And the team sucked anyway. We were solidly LAST PLACE in the league.

Our entire purpose at the games is (1) to rip tickets at the gate and (2) narc on anyone who is having more fun than we are—which is basically EVERYONE. How could it not be? We're charged with standing around looking like a bunch of geeky buttwipes, while at the same time alienating our peers. Woohoo! What a deal. I mean, let's face it, even the MARCHING BAND has cooler uniforms and more peer support than we do.

Here's the other thing I was cranked off about as I sat there in the bogus briefing: Dylan. I'd spent more time with the guy in the last ten days than he'd spent with his own girlfriend, and I wanted to despise him. I really did. But, he was making it verrrrry difficult, and that was supremo aggravating.

Dylan was absolutely everything I did not want in a guy . . . and yet, the more I hung around him, the harder it became to ignore his major hottie factor. Plus, he could be sort of nice, and he wasn't totally the cookie cutter guy I'd imagined him to be. SIGH. Get this: he actually has a tattoo of that cool striped monster from *Where the Wild Things Are* on his shoulder. I don't know WHY I found that overwhelmingly sexy (other than the fact that I'd gotten a glimpse of his bare chest, back, shoulder, and abs the same time I spied the tatt), but I did. I mean, what a sweet choice for ink!

Tattoo aside, the whole situation with us working as a team was unfair and unbalanced. I was subjected to his blinding hunkiness and intimate knowledge of his coolio tattoo every day, while he merely had an up-front and personal view of my giant butt in the heinous man pants. FAIR?!? I think not. (I can almost hear my dad's voice saying, "No one ever said life would be fair, Lila." Yeah, tell me about it.)

I was absolute guy-repellent in my junior narc costume, and no one cared. Life was miserable. Having to look that horrid in front of one of the cutest guys in school was really more than I could handle.

From day one of my sentence, though, I must say Dylan had been nothing but nice to me, even when I went out of my way to be a hag (which I did every day). I can appreciate that in a guy.

Someone ELSE'S guy, Lila. Remember?

I had to remind myself of that a lot now.

His girlfriend was none other than the illustrious Miffany's best friend and fellow cheerleader, Jennifer Hamilton. She's petite and blonde, and I can guarantee her butt does not require its own zip code. She has this whole sweetsie-blecho persona going, but I don't know. It seems more like a role she plays than who she really is. Sure she looks cute and bubbly at first glance, but she has this hard veneer you glimpse every so often when her guard is down. I mean, her *best friend* is dating my brother, and yet Jennifer's never even made direct eye contact with me. Not once. If we do pass in the hall, or whatever, her gaze moves over me as if I were a fern or some wallpaper—just there, but not worthy of her time or attention.

Regardless of my feelings about her, though, she was Dylan's girlfriend. So, no matter how nice he was to me, or how much time we spent together, no matter how kickin' his tattoo was in comparison to all the generic designs out there, Dylan Sebring was STILL Some Other Girl's Guy. I'd be an idiot to even fantasize that the situation were different, not to mention that he is not, and would never be, the least bit interested in Lila Lawbreaker Moreno, of all people.

Which is fine, because I don't want him.

[Sniff]

No, really. I don't.

Sloppy cheerleader seconds? YEEEEEECH.

My dad's robotic Mini-Me? Not so much.

My mission, hence, was to do everything in my power to show Dylan Sebring and the rest of the world that his charms did nothing for me, and I was not (even though I kinda was, but not *really*) crushing on him. Hiding my feelings would be a piece of cake, right? I have four pesky brothers. Snide disdain is an attitude I've raised to an art form out of sheer necessity.

Sound and movement suddenly burst all around me, yanking me out of my ruminations. I blinked up at the pandemonium in the "briefing room," trying to figure out what was going on. Dylan had apparently finished his stupid gung ho cop speech, because the rest of the narcs were scattering like happy little cockroaches, all bright-faced and pukingly chipper, ready to head out to Cougar Stadium.

I, on the other hand, stayed in my seat, actively practicing poor posture and apathy. Believe me, I had no urgency to get this party started.

"Excited about the game?" Lt. Oblivious-to-Body-Language asked, once we were alone in the room and he stood directly in front of me. He rubbed his palms together and smiled at me as though we had a rollicking good time ahead of us.

Of course, I thought the question had been a joke, but it looked like he really meant it. Cool tatt or not, that was one heck of a dumbass question. I glanced up with a death-glare expression. "What are you, high?"

"Aw, come on, Moreno." He reached out and tugged on a lock of my hair, which gave me chills. "It'll be fun."

I made a show of pulling away from him, scowling as I stood up, but secretly it was kind of cool how he just felt free to touch me all casual-like. Still, I couldn't let on that he affected me in any way at all.

Jennifer Hamilton. Jennifer Hamilton. Jennifer Hamilton.

That did it. My surliness quotient jumped a notch. "You have a twisted idea of fun, Sebring. What do you do for a date? Lock your girlfriend in the trunk of your car?"

He just laughed as if my fury were more amusing than a pile of puppies. Was he practicing to be my dad or something? Oh, yes. HOW could I forget? That's EXACTLY what he was doing. HORK. My resolve to resist strengthened even further.

"Look," he said, draping his arm over my shoulder as we headed for the door, "you seem nervous, but don't sweat tonight."

I shrugged his arm off, even though it had felt pretty nice there. *Step away from the Lila.* "Please," I said, with a giant scoff. "Like I am."

"Well, it is your first time on duty, so I thought—"

"Look, I prayed to the Virgin Mary about it before I got here, okay?" I said, in a sarcastic, and probably blasphemous, tone. "I think I'll muddle through."

Another laugh. To be honest, he was *annoyingly* unaffected by my venomous attitude, which was annoyingly reminiscent of my FATHER. Again. "Whatever," he said lightly. "Just hang with me and I'll walk you through everything."

"Yeah, thanks. But I really don't think I need a lesson on how to rip a ticket, Dylan. Oh, I'm sorry. I meant *Lieutenant* Sebring." I viciously yanked up my ugly parka zipper, wishing I had a deep hood in which to hide my face.

His head cocked to the side like a curious puppy, and he studied my face. "You're fun, Lila. You know that?"

My tummy jumped and got kind of warm, so I didn't say anything. But I bit the insides of my cheeks to keep from smiling, then managed a huge "whatever" eye roll.

"No, really. Most girls are just sort of . . . nice. But you're totally not. It's refreshing."

Huh?!?!? I wanted to take it as a compliment, and I'm sure he meant it that way, but he'd just told me I wasn't *nice*. SWELL. I mean, sure, I wasn't exactly trying to be nice, but still. "Gee, thanks, sweet talker." I punched him in the vicinity of his *Wild Thing* tattoo. Hard. "With lines like that, I'm surprised you don't have the girls banging down your door . . . carrying loaded shotguns."

He laughed really hard at that one. "See?" he said, all happy-camperish, flipping his hands palm up. "You're totally not nice. In fact, you're practically like one of the guys."

Greeeeeeeeeat. Now I was one of the guys. And, GOSH, lucky for me, I had the man pants to prove him right.

Why couldn't someone take me out of my misery?

I stuffed my hands into my pockets and kept my gaze directly on the wintery ground in front of me as we traipsed en masse into the fenced-in, outdoor stadium adjacent to the high school building. Huge mounds of snow from the big post-homecoming storm still piled up against the fences and sheds, and a thick white blanket of the stuff covered the hills outside the stadium. The maintenance people had done a good job of clearing the football field and bleachers, but there was still a bit of snowpack on the sidewalks. I listened to the crunch of it beneath the treads of my Rocky boots; it sounded like we were marching off to war.

I peeked out of the corner of my eye to see if Caressa and Meryl had shown up yet, but I didn't see either of them. It was wicked cold, so people had just begun to trickle in. Thanks to my double-grounding and the fact that all my time was being taken up with this awful junior narc stuff, we'd hardly had time to talk since the day after the dumb supper. I was looking forward to catching up. I was dying to know what, if anything, was up with Meryl and Ismet, and to see if Caressa had come to her senses about the CD guy.

The rockers, stoners, and rebels had begun to congregate beneath the bleachers, looking all casual and *so* not high schoolish. None of them gave a rip about the game, which I'd always found so cool. They just came to hang out in the down under with their peeps.

I released a soul-deep sigh of mourning as I studied their ripped denim, worn leather, and long hair. Surely none of those guys would ever give me a second glance now that I was a junior narc on TOP of being the chief's daughter. BIG double red flag.

Dylan and I set up shop just inside the chain link gate, at a table provided by the Booster Club. Someone's ultra-peppy mother was there with us. She was kind of annoying with her perkiness and her attempts to be "one of the kids," but otherwise pretty nice, I guess. I got the feeling she was trying to relive her own high school years through being totally involved with the boosters, which was sorta pathetic and made me feel sad for her. But, hey, at least she was involved. You sure couldn't say that about a lot of parents.

I don't know where the team was, but the band was on the field practicing our fight song. It's funny—I don't even know the real words to it, because we always change it up like this:

Cheer, cheer for White Peaks High.
You bring the whiskey, I'll bring the rye,
Send those freshman out for gin,
Don't let a sober sophomore in.
We never stumble, we never fall
We sober up on wood alcohol,
Loyal peeps of WPHS,
Step up to the bar for more!

My dad, the principal, and the superintendent— überscary Dr. Judith Cannon—all despise the fact that the entire student body practically screams those words instead of the real ones whenever we're supposed to sing along. We've even had assemblies about it, believe it or not, during which they get together, all serious-faced, and issue one big group smackdown to us.

It doesn't change anything.

Frankly, I think they ought to lighten up. The stupid song has been sung that way practically since *they* were high school age. It's not like we REALLY sober up on wood alcohol, for God's sake. I don't even know what wood alcohol is. But, the made-up lyrics are amusing, whereas the real words are so booo-o-oring.

I was standing at the table, sullenly fiddling with the fuzz inside the pockets of my parka, when Meryl and Caressa be-bopped up and sort of grabbed me.

"Thank God you guys are here." I leaned in for a group hug, then turned my butt toward them and looked back over my shoulder. "How hideous are these pants?" I whispered.

"You look really cute!" Meryl said.

I gave her a sick smile. Nice fashion sense. "Right."

"How's it going?" Caressa asked, not commenting on my garb whatsoever, which said a lot, coming from Caressa.

"It's going."

"Hi, Dylan," Meryl said, looking past me.

"Hey." He grinned. "Hi, Caressa."

"Hello." Caressa sort of jostled me from the side. "How's our little prisoner treating you?"

"Caressa!"

Dylan just laughed. "She *loves* it so far. Don't you, Moreno."

"Bite me, Sebring."

He wagged his finger and looked at me all playful-like. "Now see, you *still* haven't asked me nicely, or I just might."

ACK!!!!!

I averted my gaze. "Do you mind if I talk to my friends for a few minutes? I haven't seen them at all since I've been on house arrest." It irked the hell out of me that I had to ask permission, but he *did* have to give progress reports to my dad.

"Of course I don't care. Go on." He glanced around, then lowered his voice and pierced me with a knowing expression. "Keep in mind your dad will probably show up in a half hour or so. You might want to be over here before then."

"Oh." It felt good that he sort of had my back. It was the first glimpse I'd had of him not being a total yes man with my dad, and I liked it. "Thanks. I'll keep an eye out."

Meryl, Caressa, and I walked over to the refreshment kiosk and bought ourselves hot cocoa. We stood in a little huddle off to the side, talking to each other through the wisps of steam rising from our paper cups. There were too many people around, so we didn't bring up the dumb supper at all. It was one thing to be desperate enough for dates to conduct a metaphysical ritual like a dumb supper . . . another thing entirely to openly talk about it in front of schoolmates. So, we chatted about classes, parents, my grounding, the junior narcs. Caressa told us a little about play rehearsals (she hated them). Meryl told us all about how she'd been doing some self-study about Bosnian culture, Ramadan, and the Bosnian dialect of Serbo-Croatian that Ismet's family spoke, so she could be more respectful of his life. (That Meryl!)

After a few minutes of chatter, though, my best buddies veered off in a new direction with zero warning. "So, Lila, I totally think Hutch was flirting with you," Caressa said calmly.

I jolted. Inside my chest, a warm ball of pleasure blossomed, but I couldn't let it show. "Don't be ridiculous," I rasped. "He has a girlfriend, need I remind you.

A perky blonde cheerleader. He's only hanging out with me because he has to."

"Sure, he has to hang out with you. But he doesn't have to like it," Meryl said, raising her eyebrows in this knowing way that always makes her seem ten years more mature than the rest of us. "But he's totally liking it."

"How do you know?"

Caressa and Meryl exchanged this amused glance. "It's completely obvious," Caressa said.

I bought time sipping my hot chocolate, wondering how I would feel if Dylan really did have a thing for me. I mean, he had so many strikes against him. My surreptitious gaze strayed over toward him, but my stomach contracted sourly when I saw Jennifer Hamilton and her rah-rah posse gathered around him all worshipfully. He said something, and a burst of girlish tittering ensued. Blech.

Newsflash: those girls were *nice*.

I wasn't.

He dated them.

He supervised me. Because he *had* to.

Yeah, right. Sure, he was flirting with me. SNORT. I

turned my back on the nauseating display and addressed my friends. "Look, Hutch wouldn't even be in my galaxy if it weren't for this punishment." I leaned in and added, "He told me I was like one of the *guys*."

"He what?" Caressa shrieked.

"Yeah. It's that bad. So, let's drop it. He's not my type anyway."

"How could he not be your type?" Meryl asked. "He's hot!"

Hot, schmot. I tried to completely put Dylan out of my mind, focusing instead on one particular rocker guy I found truly hot. His name is Tristan Vallejos, which totally doesn't fit him. Why do parents saddle their kids with names like that? We have another guy in our school named Crispin, of all godawful things. He accidentally blew something up in chemistry last year, completely burning off one half of his unibrow and a sideburn. Everyone has called him Crispy Critter since, but what did his parents expect after giving him a name like that? It's no wonder he wears black all the time, even on his lips and nails, and has pierced everything but his actual eyeballs.

As for my hottie rocker, no one calls him Tristan,

thankfully, because it makes him sound like he should be a fashion expert on *Queer Eye for the Straight Guy* or something (not that I don't LOVE that show, of course). Instead, everyone calls him Zap, for Frank Zappa, who is this really ancient rock star who once recorded a song called "Broken Hearts Are for A**holes." He's famous for other stuff, but that's the only song that stuck in my head, for obvious humor-based reasons. Anyway, Zap and I had done the mild-to-moderate-flirting-with-potential thing in detention about a year ago until he realized the identity of my dear pa-pa. That ended that, but I still found him to be superyummy.

Zap stood right on the edge of the bleachers with some of his buddies, smoking a cigarette. In truth, I don't really like smoking . . . but Zap looked cool when he did it. Zap looks really exotic, with his dark complexion and long black hair. He plays in a garage band and speaks fluent Spanish. I lifted my chin toward him. "Now, THAT is my kind of guy," I told my friends.

They followed my gaze. Zap took one last drag on his cig, squinting through the smoke. He held the cig pinched between his thumb and forefinger as he blew out a smoke ring, then raised one boot to rest on the opposite knee and ground out the smoldering stub on his thick rubber soles. It was such an übercoolio move, I almost wished I smoked so I could do it, too.

"Zap's a great guitar player," Caressa said, as if she was looking for reasons to like him.

"I know." I sighed. "Dreamy."

Meryl, on the other hand, cut right to the chase. "Lila, give it up. Zap Vallejos is cute, sure, but he will never give you the time of day," she said, matter-of-factly. "Face it. Stoners frown on the idea of dating cops' daughters."

"Whatever." I pouted, but she was right. Didn't mean I wanted to admit it. I glanced at my watch. "Look, I have to get back. If my dad shows up and I'm not glued to Hutch like an artificial limb, he'll kill me."

We hugged good-bye, then Caressa and Meryl tromped up into the stands. I stopped at the kiosk and bought a refill of hot chocolate, deciding at the last minute to get one for Dylan, too. I was just trying to be thoughtful. If I was this cold, he had to be cold, too.

When I walked up to Dylan and the blonde gaggle holding the steaming cups, Jennifer Hamilton and her entourage froze in mid-titter. All their faces turned toward me, and Jennifer's smile went sort of brittle. They stared at me like I was a sex offender, fresh from jail and unleashed onto their neighborhood. It was the first time I could remember any of them looking *at* me rather than *through* me, and it made me highly uncomfortable.

"Soooo, baby," she purred to Dylan, moving closer to lay a proprietary French-manicured hand on his shoulder as she drilled me with that evil stare, "is this your new little recruit?"

Dylan sort of rolled his eyes, but Jennifer missed it. "This is Lila. Lila, this is Jennifer and . . . everyone."

"Hi," I said to them without enthusiasm before turning to Dylan with the cocoa. I would never fit in with those girls, and I didn't even want to. What did I care about being cordial? "Here," I told him. "I thought you might want this."

He took it, smiling down at me. "Hey, thanks."

The blondes exchanged a series of sucked-cheek glances.

Finally, Jennifer stepped forward, her entire group of followers sort of bolstering her from behind. "So tell me," she said, in this sharply sweet tone that ANY female would recognize as snotty and competitive, but most clueless guys mistake for just sweet, "do all the recruits serve refreshments to their superiors, or is it just the females?"

"Geez, Jen," I heard Dylan say.

I whipped a shocked glance at Jennifer, furious and ready to crack open a big ol' can of whup-ass on her for that innuendo. Why did girls like her always have to be so catty and mean to girls like me? What did *I* ever do to her?

Suddenly, though, the truth dawned on me.

I had the upper hand in this whole situation because I wasn't the one acting threatened and snitty and on the defensive. Her Royal Highness Hamilton was acting like a heinous bitch from hell because she was jealous. Of me!

How completely cool was that?

If I'd only known that all I needed was a shiny parka and man pants to get under Jennifer Hamilton's skin, I would've joined the narcs years ago. MOO HA HA HA . . . Not really.

But, still. The realization of my own infinite power so cheered me, I started looking at my future in a whole new way. I was being forced into junior narcdom and couldn't do anything to change that. True. But I could look for ways to make it tolerable . . . or even fun. Ripping tickets at football games and wearing ugly pants didn't generate the yuks for me, but making Jennifer Hamilton jealous and insecure would be more fun than the proverbial barrel of monkeys.

Fun enough, in fact, to make me move just a bit closer to Dylan and sort of flutter my lashes as I looked up at him. "We junior narcs do all kinds of nice things for each other, don't we, Dylan."

He looked baffled. She looked flamed.

And I felt better than I had in weeks.

eight

****■■****■■****■■****

caressa

The weeks dragged by like my private version of hell, with no results whatsoever in the boyfriend department for me or either of my best buds. Meryl had begun to hang out at the Hadziahmetovics' house, but it seemed like she spent more time chatting with Shefka and little Jenita than taking smooching lessons from Ismet. I don't know. I could be wrong, but it sure seemed that way from the outside looking in.

Lila had finally gotten "ungrounded," but she had to spend almost all her free time with Dylan and the rest of the Police Explorers, which was a complete bummer. I missed her. I was glad to see she'd really perked up since she realized Jennifer Hamilton was jealous of her time with Dylan, though. Meryl and I loved getting the updates from Operation Make Jennifer Seethe.

As for me, I was deep into rehearsals for the spring musical, which was due to open in March. In short? It was horrid, I hated it, I didn't want to be there.

We were working on blocking and choreography one afternoon right before Halloween, and at the same time going over some of the music. I stood in my designated spot, stage right, singing Belle with the rest of the cast and thinking I might smack one of the "townsfolk" upside the head if they sang, "Bonjour! Bonjour! Bonjour!" to me one more time.

Argh! I swear, I loved this play before I was forced to star in it against my will while watching amateurs doing the makeup. Behind the scenes, I would've been in hog heaven. As Belle, though, I was completely miserable. I didn't even like the stupid little teacup, Chip, anymore. I wanted to change his name to Shards, if you get my drift.

Plus, every time the guy playing horrid Gaston said that one part to the guy playing LeFou about Belle being "the most beautiful girl in town," all the girls in the entire cast broke character and stared eye daggers through me. I mean, please, it wasn't like I wrote the stupid words, nor was it like he was actually referring to ME, Caressa. His line referred to the character, Belle—duh. I couldn't care less about playing Belle!

My attention strayed from the music and the jealousy, and I noticed the costume crew was trying out Mark Bartlett's beast makeup, backstage in the wings. Mark's this really huge guy who seems like he should be just another defensive lineman on the football team, but he sings like an angel and is a die-hard Thespian. He's been in every production since freshman year. He seems like he's a little light in his loafers, too, if you know what I mean, but no one teases him about it because he's big enough to kick their butts if they did. Who cares if he wants to date guys, anyway? Mark is one of my favorite people in the whole school. He'll make an absolutely perfect Beast, too.

Or at least he would if *I* could do his makeup.

My mouth sort of fell open when I caught a glimpse of him. I was AGHAST. This bogus costume crew completely dropped the ball on the whole beast look. He looked like a gigantic ET with some sort of malignant back growth. I swear, a three-year-old could've done a better makeup job than these guys had.

"Caressa!"

Startled, I whipped around to face Mr. Cabbiatti, our director. His bushy brows dipped into a V in the middle of his forehead as he scowled at me.

I swallowed tightly. "I'm sorry, did you say something?"

He released this majorly dramatic sigh and let his eyes flutter shut, then pinched the bridge of his nose in between his forefinger and thumb. After a moment of silence, he drilled me with an exhausted glare. "If you'll recall, we're rehearsing the first musical number."

I tensed up, feeling superhot under my clothes from being singled out and yelled at in front of the entire group. Didn't the man watch Dr. Phil? This could scar me for life. Everyone was staring at me gleefully, and I was pretty sure no one other than Mark was on my side. Most of them actively disliked me, for no good reason that I could figure, and they were absolutely eating this up. "I-I know."

"Well, if you know," he said snottily, "then perhaps you could sing along to your part."

I heard some muffled laughter off to my left, but I just lifted my chin and ignored whoever it was. I was used to it, but it still hurt. "I'm sorry."

"Can you keep your mind in the here and now, please?"

NO, I wanted to say. No, I can't keep my mind in the here and now, because I don't want to be *here, now* or ever. I either wanted to be backstage fixing that stupendously pathetic makeup job on the Beast, or I wanted to be home with my friends, thinking up ways to meet Bobby Slade.

But I was stuck. My parents didn't believe in quitting something once you'd committed, and even though I hadn't WANTED to commit, they were unsympathetic. They didn't get it. I'd explained my predicament of having been railroaded until I was hoarse, but it looked like I would be reading and singing the part of Belle in the stupid play, like it or not.

I blinked away a stinging feeling in my eyes and smoothed my damp palms down the sides of my jeans. "I'm sorry. Can we just start again?"

Mr. Cabbiatti—whom all of us called Mr. CRABbiatti or The Crab because of his bipolar mood swings during productions—crossed his arms and huffed. He could never just let anything go. And the funny thing was, during off-times, when no one was rehearsing for anything, Cabbiatti was one of the coolest teachers out there. But he started pulling the "Mommy Dearest" act almost immediately after any cast list was posted. It was sort of like he thought a big-time director was supposed to behave that way, so he did. Someone needed to remind the guy he was the theater director in White Peaks High School, White Peaks, Colorado, for Pete's sake.

Small freakin' potatoes.

"You know, Caressa," he started in, which made me brace myself for the worst, "your father will be at the play opening night, I'm sure. You wouldn't want to slaughter a song in front of the legendary Tibby Lee."

I heard barely stifled groans coming from the same vicinity that the laughter had come from earlier, and my heart sank. Just great. Everyone acted like *I* was throwing my famous dad into their faces, when I hadn't mentioned a thing. How many times did I have to tell people, he's just *my dad*? Why did this always happen to me? God! I didn't flaunt *anything*, much less my parents. To be frank, I spent a lot of energy trying to HIDE the identity of my father, just to make my school life tolerable.

Then, along came people like The Crab.

I blew out an exasperated breath and flicked my hand toward Crabbiatti, but my chin quivered ever so slightly when I spoke. I had enough trouble fitting in with my peers without some wannabe Steven Spielberg making it harder for me. "Fine. I'm sorry. Let's just do it again. Okay?" I hoped no one had seen evidence that The Crab had gotten under my skin.

"Don't get snippy, young lady."

"I'm—" *not*, I started to say, feeling the need to defend myself. But why bother? I clamped my lips shut, crossed my arms, then waited for him to restart the song. When he finally did, I sang the words by rote and with absolutely no feeling or spark. I was totally the rice cake of actresses right then—dry, boring, zero "flavah."

The only thing I could think of was Bobby Slade, and I focused on him for the rest of rehearsal in an effort to ignore the awful, yet sadly familiar, feeling of being ostracized. What did I care about these kids when I had Bobby to look forward to? (Okay, I kinda cared. I couldn't help it.) Junior prom was in May, which was only seven months away. I needed to figure something out ASAP, or I'd never meet the guy in time to fall madly in love—

Wait a minute!

My heart started to pound and my palms grew moist. If Crabbiatti and the rest of them insisted on using my famous dad against me, maybe this one time I could use my famous dad for my benefit! Wasn't it only fair? An idea so stupendous blossomed in my head, I couldn't wait to run it by Lila. I checked my watch; forty-five minutes until I could leave rehearsals and share my brilliant brainstorm.

It was so simple!

Why hadn't I thought of it weeks ago??

Lila

I'd been a junior narc for almost a month, and my life hadn't ended. Sometimes that still surprised me. Don't get me wrong—I still loathed the thick polyester get-up with the white-hot fiery passion of a thousand burning suns, but I enjoyed making Jennifer Hamilton squirm so much that it kind of made up for having to wear it. One part of me felt bad that she seemed to take out her oh-so-unattractive insecurity on Dylan, but hey, since when did I need to coddle Mr. Dad Clone? He'd have to fend for himself, much like I'd been forced to do.

We'd just finished a stupid training on defensive tactics and Dylan and I were walking out of the building together. Although I grumbled, I actually liked defensive tactics, which was a big, fancy title meaning "how to royally kick someone's butt while avoiding having your own kicked." Hey, if my dad approved of me learning this stuff, who was I to argue? I frankly looked forward to using some of the cool moves I'd perfected on Luke the Puke.

Dylan had offered to give me a ride home, and since I DIDN'T HAVE A CHANCE IN HELL OF EVER DRIVING MYSELF, THANK YOU, FATHER, I'd taken him up on it. To my surprise, though, Caressa was waiting outside the police station, idling away in her little Beemer. It was a relief to see her.

Sometimes when Dylan drove me home, there was this weird tension in the car. It's hard to explain. I mean, we chatted and sniped at each other and stuff like normal, but, there was this creepy less-than-comfortable edge to it all. It was kind of like how it feels when someone farts in public, and everyone knows it but, by unspoken agreement, everyone totally ignores the fart and just goes on like nothing happened. Know what I mean? Totally fake and uncomfortable.

Anyway, I was more than happy to see Caressa waiting for me. A little beepity-beep-beep sounded from her horn, and she waved. I waved back, then turned toward Dylan. "Hey, I'll see you later, okay? I'll catch a ride home from Caressa. My house is on the way to hers."

He shrugged. "Sure, whatever. Hey, Lila," he called, after I'd jogged off. I turned back. "You did good today."

The comment made me feel warm and fuzzy, but I worked up a prodigious scoff and spread my arms wide. I continued walking backward toward Caressa. "Yeah, because I was going to lose sleep over it if I sucked. Have a clue much, Dylan?" I formed my thumb and forefinger into an L shape and smacked it onto my forehead. "Lila does not CARE about the junior narcs or any of the dumb classes that go with being one."

He laughed, as always unduly cheered by my snarkiness. "Whatever. I'll see you at school."

"Not if I see you first," I retorted. Had to maintain my not-nice status, after all, or he might think I was going all cheerleader on him. GAG.

I hurled myself into the safety of Caressa's BMW 325xi and pulled the seatbelt across my body. "Hey, woman." I grinned. "I didn't expect to see you here."

"Yeah, I . . . thought I'd try to catch you."

She seemed nervous, which piqued my curiosity big time. I swiveled in my seat to face her. "What's up, pup?"

Caressa bit her bottom lip for a minute, studying my face. Finally, she said, "I have a favor to ask you," in this timid, totally non-Caressa tone of voice.

"Okay." Color me baffled. "Shoot."

Her words came in a big jumble. "I don't want you to think I'm trying to get you in trouble, though. You know I wouldn't do that. Plus, I'll give you a full manicure and pedicure if you do this for me. I just got that new OPI shade you liked in the magazine, *It's Greek to Me.*"

Now I was really intrigued. "Just tell me, Caressa!"

"Okay, okay." She gave me another nervous grin and raised her eyebrows. "I've figured out a way to meet Bobby Slade."

Inside, I groaned. HELLO, it was mid-October. It had been WEEKS since the dumb supper, and Caressa still hadn't given up on the Bobby Slade nonsense. I gave her this big-eyed sarcastic look. "Okaay, but what does that have to do with me?"

"I need your expertise."

I glanced around the car to make sure she was talking to me. "Newsflash, loco one, I have no expertise with meeting regular guys, much less famous musicians."

"Not that kind of expertise."

"Then what? Spit it out."

"Don't say no right away."

"Caressa!"

"Okay! Sheesh!" She sucked in a big breath, then eased it slowly out her nose, meditation-style. With slightly shaky hands, she reached for a large manila envelope that I hadn't noticed sitting on the dashboard, undid the little metal clasp, and slipped out a letter . . . typed on her dad's letterhead.

I grabbed it. "What the heck is this?" I asked, unnecessarily. I mean, I could read the thing myself. DUH. I skimmed through it, then frowned up at my jittery friend with a startled expression. THIS I had not expected. "Your dad wants to produce Bobby Slade's next single? Wow, talk about a weird freakin' coincidence."

"It's actually sort of . . . not true."

Confused, I blinked at her and then held up the letter and kind of waggled it. "But, he wrote—"

"I wrote it."

"Huh?"

She bit one corner of her bottom lip. "My dad knows nothing about this. That's where you come in."

I rolled my hand impatiently so she'd give me the full 411 ALL AT ONCE. This was like pulling teeth.

She clasped her hands together, imploring me. "You've got to do this for me, Lila. I'll die if you don't."

"WHAT?!?"

"Forge my dad's signature on the letter."

My jaw dropped open, and I gaped at her cringing expression.

"Please? Pretty, pretty please?"

"Are you trying to get me sent off to juvie?"

"Lila, no one will know. It's not related to school, so you can't get expelled or anything. Pleeeeeease?"

"Forget expulsion. What about my dad?"

"Come on, how's he ever going to find out."

How, indeed? The risk-taker in me weakened and took the bait. I reread the letter, then looked up into Caressa's overly bright, crushingly hopeful face. I couldn't say no to her. I mean, I would never voice this to her, but what were the odds something could come of this? I felt quite certain that Bobby Slade's managers or whoever would skim the letter, come to the instant conclusion it was bogus (not to mention lame), and round-file the thing without even responding. Bobby himself would probably never even see it.

At the risk of repeating myself, he is a famous musician! HELLO!!

Besides, I'm sure if Tibby Lee wanted to produce someone's single, HIS people would call THEIR people and *blah, blah, blah* . . . lunches would be had, martinis would be downed. I mean, what the heck do I know about how musical deals happen? *Nada*. But my sense was, there wouldn't be a letter at all.

I narrowed my gaze. Might as well lay down some ground rules before I potentially signed my freedom away. "Do you promise, if I sign this, that you'll stop your nutso, stalkerish preoccupation with Bobby? I mean, if something comes of it"—*yeah sure*—"then fine. I'll even say you were right and I was wrong. But until then, you have to promise to let it go and see what fate has in store. AND, you have to start looking at guys our age and within our universe."

Caressa clapped and bounced in her seat. "Fine, yes, whatever. Just sign it."

"Promise, Caressa."

"I promise!"

"Swear on something important!"

"I swear on something important!" She laughed. "Just kidding. I swear on . . . Sephora.com."

My brows shot up. Whoa. She really *was* serious if she swore on THAT. I held out my palm and snapped my fingers inward with feigned impatience. "Give me a pen, then. Make it quick."

"You won't regret this, Lila." She fished in her handbag, then handed over a pen. "I promise."

"Ha. I regret it right now. I don't have a license or a car fund-matching deal, and I'm wearing man pants, thanks to my last foray into forgeryland, if you'll recall." I scribbled down Mr. Thibodoux's signature, which was firmly implanted in my brain files. "But I'll do anything to bring you back from the brink of Bobby Slade psychosis. Plus I'm going to deny ever having done this if it comes down to it."

"That's okay. I'll back you up."

I finished, checked my work—which was perfect as always—then handed the letter over. "There. Now drive me home. I've got to get out of this repulsive outfit before I freak out."

Caressa giggled. She slipped the letter carefully back into the envelope, set it aside, then put her car into drive and pulled away from the curb. As we drove off, she flicked me a mischievous glance. "So. Dylan was looking hot back there."

God, not again. I rolled my eyes. I SO didn't want to get into this beating-a-dead-horse conversation. "And I'm sure Jennifer Hamilton cares," I snarked. "Good thing I don't."

I turned toward the window and focused on a little herd of elk—who were getting superfuzzy for the winter—grazing by the road. I had to. If I'd looked directly at Caressa, she'd have seen the lie in my expression.

Okay, okay, I was warm for Dylan's form.

That DIDN'T mean I planned on doing anything about it!!

nine

* ▪ * ▪ * ▪ *

meryl

There were good aspects and bad aspects to my post—dumb supper life. On the good side: Ismet and I had sort of become friends since the big flat tire/epiphany night. On the bad side: every time I started to think that maybe he liked me, too—in THAT way—he'd do something to remind me, in no uncertain terms, that I was fooling myself. Ismet Hadziahmetovic didn't have any romantic interest in me whatsoever. When I said we were *friends*, I meant it literally.

Buddies, pals, school friends. It really was depressing.

I mean, I suppose he simply wasn't attracted to skinny, pale, tragically unhip, blue-eyed redheads with freckles. But I was really, REALLY attracted to him, and I just wanted it to be reciprocal. Was that too much to ask? I couldn't help my genetic make up. Redheads need love, too.

Despite the depressing lack of romantic action on the Ismet front, however, I'd still managed to become a frequent guest at the Hadziahmetovics' house. Not as Ismet's girlfriend (bad part) but because I'd begun to tutor Shefka in Spanish (a good part, despite the no-Ismet deal). Initially, I'd agreed to the tutoring thinking it would be a foot in the door, literally. But soon I counted Shefka as one of my friends, and our friendship didn't hinge on her brother at all. The more I visited, the more I came to enjoy hanging around the whole Hadziah-metovic family, especially their little sister, Jenita, who was seven and adorable. Plus, tutoring Shefka was a breeze, and it was keeping my Spanish skills fresh.

Shefka already spoke the Bosnian dialect of Serbo-Croatian, English, and Russian, and she could hold her own in Turkish. If our study sessions were any indica-tion, she would soon be fluent in Spanish as well. To say she had a real knack for foreign languages was a gross understatement. The best part of our budding friend-ship, though, was the long, interesting conversations we shared about what it was like living in Sarajevo and how it felt to leave permanently.

After every tutoring session, Shefka and I would sit around and talk about her homeland while little Jenita stood behind me putting sparkly butterfly clips and various ponytail holders in my hair. (She was absolutely enthralled with my stick-straight, bright red locks, and I was happy to let her style it.)

I'd been doing my own studying about Bosnian life, but hearing details from someone who'd actually lived there was invaluable. Shefka explained how there are actually three languages spoken in Bosnia—Bosnian, Serbian, and Croatian—but that most people could get by speaking any of them. We also discussed the ongoing political arguments surrounding the languages: what they should be called and so forth. I was totally intrigued by it all.

I learned that many Bosnians spoke either Russian or Turkish or both, in addition to their native languages. That blew my mind. I was glad my parents had pressed me to learn other languages, because I was happily fluent in Spanish and getting better in German every day. Don't get me wrong—I don't think I'm better than anyone because I speak foreign languages, I'm just glad I do.

The widely accepted American belief that we didn't need to speak anything except English in the U.S. was embarrassing to me, especially around people from other countries who came here to study. I felt like I needed to explain the American reluctance to learn other languages, and yet I could think of no good reason for it.

Ethnocentricity? Ignorance?

I mean, most of my peers barely spoke proper English, and if they were bilingual, their second language was something like Pig Latin. That was a generalization, of course. We do have quite a few Spanish speakers at WPHS. But, still. They take all kinds of flak for wanting to speak both English and Spanish, which frustrates me. It's dumb!

But, I digress.

In addition to language stuff, Shefka shared a lot with me about how it was living in a war zone. Snipers Alley, for example, is a street riddled with craters from the shells that rained down on it when Sarajevo was under attack. Shefka told me they paint some of the craters red, always to mark the exact spot where a passing civilian was struck down. These memorial craters are called "roses."

It made me sad for her and all the Bosnians, but it also put things into perspective for me. You never think of regular old teenagers like Ismet and Shefka living in war-torn regions, but they do. And little kids like Jenita, too. She probably didn't remember much, but even so. Sometimes, we Americans don't have a clue how lucky we are. Myself included. We take everything for granted. Safety, privileges, wealth, food, shelter—even HOPE.

Get this: Apparently the famous eternal flame in Sarajevo wasn't as eternal as it could've been. Sometimes the government had to turn it off because they couldn't afford to keep it running. They turned OFF an *eternal flame*. I can't imagine how that made the people feel, especially in the midst of war and instability.

Anyway, I loved talking to Shefka about Bosnia, and I loved the attention little Jenita showed me. I always tried to draw Ismet into our discussions, but he wasn't nearly as forthcoming about his past. At first I put his reluctance down to guy-versus-girl communication-style differences, but the longer it went on, the less sure I became. Maybe it wasn't talking about Bosnia that spurred his aversion, maybe it was talking about Bosnia *to me.* Maybe it was talking to me, *period.*

Depressing thought.

In fact, the whole Ismet deal started to really get me down after a while. I decided I needed a break from the constant rejection, so I made up an excuse about having to write a research paper and told Shefka we'd resume tutoring in two weeks or so. Jenita cried when she heard I'd be away for a while, which was sweet. But I had to do it. I needed time to clear my head and come to terms with the fact that Ismet wasn't the least bit interested in me. I wanted to be okay just being ME again. I suppose I'd been expecting things to happen with Ismet on my terms, within my time frame, and so on. That was my downfall. I was learning quickly, you just couldn't force fate. I decided to let go and see if my luck would turn around.

The first few days of avoiding him went well, but then I got the Ismet email that weakened my resolve and made me rethink my evasiveness:

FROM: USAguy@whitepeakshigh.co.edu
TO: MerylM@Morgensternfamily.com

SUBJECT: Wednesday afternoon
TIME: 4:45:03 P.M., MST

Hi Meryl,

How's the paper going? I know you're busy, but do you want to come over tomorrow after school and check out some old TRLs with me, Shefka, and Jenita? My friend gave them to me. We have not seen you for a while, so we thought it would be fun.

Ismet

I was so thrilled by the invitation to go hiking, I barely noted how strange it was to see Ismet use an abbreviation—TRLs—instead of writing out *trails*. I gave it a brief "huh" kind of thought and then blew it off as a quirk. I quickly wrote back and accepted.

It wasn't technically a date considering it would be all four of us, but I didn't mind. Shefka was as much a friend as Ismet, if not more, and we all liked hanging around Jenita, who was the happiest, most optimistic kid I'd ever met. The fact that Ismet had reached out was the important point. It showed me that letting go had worked. He and I would be spending time together—that's all that mattered!

I didn't really understand the part about his friend giving him the trails, but I figured he meant that his friend TOLD HIM about the trails. He did have some idiomatic challenges with English now and then (which was SO adorable).

I didn't mention the invitation to Lila and Caressa, because I didn't want to jinx myself. I decided to just believe that things were looking up in the Ismet department, and I went on my happy-go-lucky way. DUH.

In typical Meryl fashion, I had been reading up on Ramadan, which I knew was the ninth month of the Muslim calendar and started on October twenty-seventh this year—in just a few days. I found the custom fascinating and decided I'd ask Shefka and Ismet more about it while we hiked. I mean, they would have to fast for a month! At least whenever the sun was up. During Ramadan, Muslims were only allowed to eat or drink after the sun went down. How did you keep from eating or drinking during daylight for a whole month? I wondered if Jenita had to participate too, and I assumed the answer was yes. It had to be even harder for a kid.

From talking to Shefka, I knew the Hadziahmetovics were very liberal in their Muslim beliefs and practices, but they did celebrate Ramadan. Discussing this most important religious holiday would show them, hopefully, how much I respected their culture and differences. Once Ismet realized that I was truly interested in him and his heritage, he'd eventually come to view me in a more romantic light. That was my theory, at least.

Who wouldn't want that when they were in a new country?

I mean, a lot of the girls in school still referred to him as That Bosnian Guy, without any respect at all for his individuality. They even made fun of his supersexy accent, which annoyed me.

Social cliques were ridiculous, and the whole "who-is-boyfriend-material" thing struck me as rigid and idiotic. It seemed that most girls my age just wanted generic American guys who fit certain sports and popularity profiles, regardless of whether they were decent people or not. Those girls wouldn't give Ismet—or anyone different—the time of day.

Which, come to think of it, was WAY better for me.

The last thing I needed was a bunch of competition.

The afternoon of the hike, I hurried home from school and bundled myself up against the weather. I wore my expedition-weight long underwear, fleece, outer shell, ski pants, gaiters, hat, gloves, and my winter hiking boots and YakTrax. Hiking the Rocky Mountains in winter was great fun as long as you were properly dressed for the conditions.

I got to the Hadziahmetovics' house at about three, and knocked on the door. Ismet answered, and he looked at me in surprise. "Cold?"

I laughed. "No, but I don't want to freeze on the trails. I'm wearing layers." On that note, I checked his outfit. Jeans, a short-sleeved T-shirt, no shoes. Huh. And they said girls were bad about being ready on time. All I knew was, he had better get a move on, or we'd run out of daylight.

His surprise turned into bewilderment. "Trails?"

I frowned slightly. It was my turn to be confused. "Well . . . yeah. I thought we were going hiking." I peered past him. "Where are Shefka and Jenita? Are they ready?"

"Ready? For . . . did you say hiking?"

"Um . . . yeah." Why was he acting so spacey?

He hitched his thumb over his shoulder. "But what about the TRLs?"

"That's what I mean."

His expression relaxed. "Oh. Good. I have the VCR all set up and Shefka is making popcorn with Jenita."

"Ismet, you're not making sense. What about hiking on the old trails your friend told you about?"

"Huh?"

For a moment, we both stood there staring at each other, then my heart started to pound out a dull warning thud in my chest. Oh, God. Clearly we'd had some sort of communication breakdown, and I had a feeling it was all on my part and I was about to be really embarrassed.

Ismet scratched his head and sort of squinted his eyes apologetically at me. "Meryl, I am thinking we are talking about different things."

"Yeah, I . . ." I shook my head. " . . . I may have misunderstood you, I guess."

"Come on in." He stepped aside.

I walked into the house, unzipping my coat and pulling off my hat and gloves. I was hot from being overdressed, but also from feeling like an idiot. I didn't have access to a mirror, but I could bet my complexion was that hideous blotchy red.

"So, I don't know what you are talking about with the hiking, but I have borrowed tapes of some of the best TRL episodes. You know, from MTV?" He waited. I made no acknowledgment. "So . . . I thought we could all watch them." He gave me a funny smile, almost as if he were on the brink of laughing at me. "What did you think I was talking about?"

Television. I should've known.

TRLs wasn't an abbreviation for trails. It was . . . something else about which I had NO clue.

I stood there, suffocating on my own mortification, and realized it was the first time in more than a decade that I felt ashamed for the way my family and I lived. That, in turn, made me feel AWFUL. I was humiliated by my own cluelessness, though, and I really, really didn't want Ismet to think I was strange. Then I felt guilty for even WORRYING that someone—anyone—would disagree with my lifestyle or make fun of me for it. That wasn't ME. I felt like a sellout of the worst kind.

While my mind continued to race, I opened my

mouth to say something, although I didn't know what. Nothing came out.

Just then, Shefka rounded the corner. "*Hola*, Meryl!"

"Hi," I said, sounding sort of dazed and out of breath. I even forgot to answer her in Spanish, which was our usual pattern in order to practice conversation skills.

Jenita bounded into the room and threw her arms around me. "Meryl, you are here!"

I didn't even hug poor little Jenita back or reply to her. I was too stunned still.

Shefka's smile faded as Jenita pulled away and looked up at me with big troubled eyes.

"Are you okay?" Shefka asked.

My throat tightened. To my horror, I felt dangerously close to bursting into tears. I shook my head. My voice quavered slightly when I said, "I . . . I just remembered something I was supposed to do for my mom." I flipped my hand over sort of helplessly. "I'm sorry."

"Wait. You have to leave?" Ismet asked, seeming more baffled than ever. "What about the shows?"

"Don't go, Meryl!" Jenita cried.

I started backing toward the door, because I was

afraid I might lose it right then and there. It was such a strange reaction for me. If this was what it meant to have a crush on a guy, then count me out. "I don't know. I have to . . . I'm sorry."

"Jenita, come here." Shefka said, in a low tone. The little girl obeyed. "Don't worry, Meryl," Shefka added, looking like she might understand more than she was letting on. I mean, she'd been to my house once. Maybe she'd noticed the distinct lack of televisions and had put two and two together. Probably not. I didn't know!

I think she had an idea that I had a crush on her brother, though, and surely she knew it wasn't reciprocated. I had no way of really knowing what was going through Shefka's mind, to be honest, and I didn't have the stomach to stand around any longer and speculate. I couldn't handle the prospect of seeing pity on any of their faces.

Jenita buried her face in the side of her big sister's sweater. I hated that I might have scared or hurt her, but it couldn't be helped.

"I'm sorry for the mix-up about the plans," Ismet said, his voice sort of uncertain.

"No. It's okay. M-my fault. I'll . . . see you both at school. Bye, Jenita."

Before any of them could say anything more, I turned heel and ran like a frightened rabbit. It's not that I was afraid that a little television watching would reach inside me and suck my brain out. I just choose to live without it, and I didn't want to compromise my convictions. I mean, Caressa and Lila and I did fine together without ever having turned on the television. If they wanted to watch something special, it was simply understood that they didn't invite me, and I was completely okay with that.

Somehow, though, thanks to my embarrassment, I hadn't been able to stand up for my beliefs and choices in front of Ismet, which made me feel weak and fraudulent. Did I really care what he, or any guy, thought? And how did I even know *how* he would've reacted? Maybe it wouldn't have even been a big deal. I bit my lip as I drove away, smearing away the tears that ran freely down my face and blurred my vision. I didn't have answers to my own questions.

I mean, what girl in her right mind would set herself up to be rejected by her number-one crush? Then again, who wants to pretend to be someone she's not just to snare a guy? GOD! It was all so confusing. The more I knew about this dating stuff, the more I wanted to go live in a cave with dogs.

When I got home, I raced up to my computer and emailed Lila and Caressa:

FROM: MerylM@Morgensternfamily.com
TO: LawBreakR@hipgirlnet.org, Lipstickgrrrrl@hipgirlnet.org
SUBJECT: S.O.S—LIFE SUCKS!!!!!!!
TIME: 3:48:14 P.M., MST

I am having the WORST DAY IN THE WORLD!!!!!!!!!! I just made a fool of myself in front of Ismet. UGH UGH! I don't want to talk about it yet, but just tell me this: what the hell is TRL????

:-((((Meryl

FROM: LawBreakR@hipgirlnet.org
TO: MerylM@Morgensternfamily.com, Lipstickgrrrrl@hipgirlnet.org
SUBJECT: re: S.O.S—LIFE SUCKS!!!!!!!
TIME: 3:50:51 P.M., MST

Uh-oh, Mer. Sounds bad! (((((((((((Meryl)))))))))))))
As for your mondo-baffling question, TRL is a televi-

sion show on MTV (which stands for Music Television—
they show music videos and stuff) where . . . um, it's
hard to explain. It's filmed on the street, sort of, in NYC,
and they have pop stars and bands and stuff come on to
be interviewed and perform. It's really cool, if you're
into television and pop stars and all that stuff you aren't
into.

But, why do you want to know??? Does this have
something to do with the debate team? Is Ismet on the
debate team? Whatever it is, don't sweat it!!! You're
fine, Mer. We love you just as you are.

xoxoxoxo—Lila

Friends 4ever!

FROM: Lipstickgrrrrl@hipgirlnet.org
TO: MerylM@Morgensternfamily.com,
LawBreakR@hipgirlnet.org
SUBJECT: re: S.O.S—LIFE SUCKS!!!!!!!
TIME: 4:05:22 P.M., MST

Meryl, girl, WHAT on earth HAPPENED???? Lila
already told you about TRL, so I won't waste the
space. But, fill us in! I hate to hear you sounding so
upset. If Ismet said something awful to you, I'll kick

his butt!!! I love you, too. ((((((((((MER))))))))))

Your best friend forever, Caressa

FROM: MerylM@Morgensternfamily.com
TO: LawBreakR@hipgirlnet.org, Lipstickgrrrrl@hip-girlnet.org
SUBJECT: re: S.O.S—LIFE SUCKS!!!!!!!—update
TIME: 4:11:59 P.M., MST

Hi Guys—

[SIGH] I've calmed down some, I think. Sorry for the panic, but I was fresh from the humiliation, and I really needed to talk to you both RIGHT THEN. And no, Caressa, Ismet didn't say anything mean to me. I just made a fool of myself because I misunderstood something he'd invited me to do. It had to do with this TRL— little did I know!!

I don't usually let that stuff bother me, but with Ismet, it did.

Slight change of subject, girls. I'm just starting to feel like the dumb supper was TRULY DUMB, as in STU-PID. Maybe I was completely off base when I said I thought it worked. I mean, all Lila does is snipe at Dylan, and he has a perky blonde girlfriend anyway.

Ismet isn't interested in me IN THE LEAST. And Caressa, you with your famous twenty-one-year-old musician thing—enough said. It's just not turning out like I know it would have if the dumb supper had worked its magic!

Maybe it didn't work after all. I don't know. Don't mind me. I'm rambling. Thanks for the hugs, both of you. I'm going to go read or meditate or eat chocolate or cry (again!) or something. I'll see you at school tomorrow.

Love, Meryl

A few minutes after I'd signed off, the phone rang. It was Shefka. I didn't want to talk to her, but when I tried to pretend I wasn't home, my mom looked at me like I'd lost my mind. So, I released this big sigh and just took the cordless phone from her. I'd have to face Shefka sooner or later.

"Are you okay?" Shefka asked, after the hello part.

"I'm fine," I lied. "I'm . . . sorry I ran out like that. Is Jenita okay?" I bit my bottom lip.

"She was disappointed to see you go, but she is fine."

I sat down on my bed, leaned against the upholstered

headboard, then crossed my legs. "I was just embarrassed is all. I didn't mean to upset her. Or you."

"But, why were you embarrassed?"

"It's a long story."

"Ismet told me about your conversation. He has no idea what's going on. Clueless boy." She paused. "Can I ask you, is this something about the television show?"

"Yeah." I sighed. "It is." I spent a few minutes explaining the way my family lives, and just like I knew she would, Shefka asked polite and intelligent questions and wasn't the least bit judgmental.

"I wish you would have just said something to me, though. It is not such a big deal."

I sighed again—something I'd been doing a lot of. It was like I lived inside a Jane Austen book or something where everyone was basically sad and dissatisfied. "I would've, but I was caught off guard in front of your brother."

Again, she lapsed into a small silence. "You like Ismet, don't you?"

Panic zinged through me briefly, but I couldn't lie. I bonked my head against my headboard. Thank goodness it was padded, or I might've suffered permanent damage. "Ugh. Am I that transparent?"

She laughed. "Not to him, if that is what worries you. You know how boys are."

"Clueless."

"Yes. Especially my brother. But, I had an idea of your feelings. I could tell by the way you look at him."

I hoped she didn't feel like I was using her to get closer to Ismet. I needed to make it clear to her, because I abhorred hurting people. "I do have a crush on Ismet, but that's not why I spend time with you and Jenita. I hope you know that."

"Of course. No need to worry. But, I guess I should tell you a few things about Ismet." She sounded almost apologetic.

My stomach contracted with something ice cold that felt like fear. What could she possibly say? Was he dying of a terminal illness? Was he gay? Was he promised in marriage to some waifish girl from Bosnia? Madly in love with a Turkish pop star? I braced myself. "Um. Okay, what?"

"Well, as much as I am proud of being Bosnian, Ismet is . . . the opposite."

"What?" Shock riddled through me.

"Yes. Since we moved here, he wants to be the all-American boy, with all-American clothes and music . . . and"—she paused, and I held my breath—"an all-American girlfriend."

UGH. Of course. "Why?" I sort of whispered.

"I do not really know. But, he is pretty . . . how do you say? *Swayed?* By the popular culture," she said. "He wants to fit in that way. And he wants a girlfriend who can help him fit in."

Which meant he didn't want ME.

I can't even tell you how disappointed I was to hear this about my number-one crush. One thing I'd never be able to do was help someone fit in with the popular culture. As if. "Great." I swallowed thickly. "I'm just what he doesn't want—a girl who knows diddly-squat about all that stuff."

Shefka made a regretful sound, but she didn't sugar-coat her reply. "I think, probably not, Meryl. At least not now while he is being struck by the stars."

I smiled a little, in spite of my mood. "Starstruck?"

"Yes, that is what I meant." Another hitch in the conversation. "I'm sorry. If it is any consolation, I think you are sweeter than any of the girls Ismet fancies from school."

Ismet was interested in girls from school?

A sour swirl of jealousy moved through my middle. I did not EVEN want to know their names. "It doesn't matter," I lied in this brittle, fake-cheery tone. I felt a resurgence of the tears I'd shed earlier. "Really. I don't *need* a boyfriend." Shefka didn't say anything, because she probably knew I was lying to myself. "Can you do me a favor, though, Shefka?"

"Sure. What?"

"Don't tell your brother I have a crush on him." I crinkled my nose at the mere thought. "I'll get over it."

"Well, all is not lost. You never know. Ismet might come around eventually."

Yeah. Sure. And I would suddenly turn into a hip and cool girl just like that—*abracadabra*. "Whatever. I mean, if he does, that's fine. I still don't want him to know how I feel."

"Will you continue to visit our house?" She sounded pensive, almost frightened of my answer.

I smiled—a bittersweet kind of a smile. Shefka was a good friend. "Of course I will. I'd miss you and Jenita too much if I didn't. Plus, I'm still your Spanish tutor."

"Good. Ismet does consider you a friend, you know."

I rolled my eyes toward the ceiling. "Well . . . great. Friends." I swallowed past the lump in my throat. "That's a good thing."

Yeah, sure it was.

It pretty much boiled down to this: Lila was one of the guys, I was a "good friend," and Caressa? Temporarily deluded. I decided right then and there that the dumb supper had indeed been a colossal failure, pointing all three of us toward the absolute MOST wrong guys ever.

They'd never like us. We'd never date them.

Our prom night dreams were a bust.

We were dateless, *still*, and firmly back at square one.

That, as they say, was that.

ten

*■ *■ *■ *

Fall dragged on like a particularly wicked case of PMS, leaving all three of us cranky, bloated with disappointment, and basically despising all things male. Despite our aspirations, nothing good had happened to any of us so far this year. No brilliant ideas, no progress in the dating department, no demonstrable improvement in our social lives—*nada*.

Big shocker of the millennium (not)—Caressa never heard anything back after she sent off that expertly forged letter to Bobby Slade. She was actually surprised by that fact, whereas the rest of us were hoping the lack of feedback would be the lightbulb inside her head to make her realize, *Hey, Bobby Slade is all wrong for me, what with him being OLD and me being MAJOR JAILBAIT.*

Why didn't I see it before? It didn't work that way for Caressa at all. She was still convinced her destiny was as Mrs. Bobby Slade. Whazzup?

Though she'd promised me on the afternoon I'd forged Mr. Thibodoux's siggy that she would quit stalking the twenty-one-year-old and start fishing in the pond of available guys our age, she had yet to cast a single line. Then again, she was pretty swamped with the dismal play rehearsals, so I decided not to issue a smackdown. It wasn't like Meryl or I were really out there baiting hooks either.

Speaking of Meryl, the whole Ismet deal had pretty much gone down the crapper. She had gotten a lot less optimistic about her prospects with the guy after it looked like his goal in life was to pretend he was an all-American boy with a starring role on *The O.C.*, instead of grasping hold of the reality that (1) he was and always would be Bosnian, which was (2) perfectly OKAY—duh, and (3) his family had unfortunately moved him to freakin' White Peaks, Colorado, not Orange County, California.

NEWSFLASH: LIFE IS NOT A TV SHOW.

HELLO! Was everyone in this town perpetually stoned?

Meryl was still gaga over the guy, though, and she spent a goodly portion of her time pining away for him and their missed potential like a freakin' war bride. She just couldn't think of an effective way to show him she was right for him, and the rest of us had begun to think maybe she wasn't.

I, in contrast to the delusions of Meryl and Caressa, had my feet firmly grounded in reality. Okay, so I still had a crush on Dylan, aka he-who-is-completely-wrong-for-me, but he was still dating Jennifer Hellspawn Hamilton. This was a fact I had fully and easily accepted, therefore I had not and would not act on my insane attraction. I was, instead, working off my tension by doing everything possible to make Hellspawn jealous.

It was child's play, really.

Jennifer had nothing on me . . . well, except for the good looks, the popularity, the hot guy, *blah blah blah*. But in the wits department, I was battling with a woefully unarmed opponent, which was a beautiful thing. She despised me, but hey, that didn't change the fact that I got to spend tons of quality time with her boyfriend while she pouted at home. Ha freakin' ha! I know that sounds evil, but if anyone deserved to be taunted, it was her.

By the big weekend after Thanksgiving, my pals and I had pretty much written off ever having meaningful relationships of any kind with the opposite sex. I had also written off the possibility of ever looking cool in front of my peers, because once again, I was forced into very visible junior narcdom. Yes, it's true. I had to work at the famous White Peaks Christmas Market looking like a public-relations dweeb of the first order.

The big annual Christmas Market went down for the full weekend after Turkey Day. It started Friday night with the tree-lighting ceremony, ice skating on the lake, a bonfire, hay rides, and copious mulled-cider consumption, not to mention midnight bikini skiing for your real hardcore types. People from all over the state (not to mention Wyoming and New Mexico) flocked to White Peaks for the festivities, spending the weekend shopping, listening to live music, watching ski exhibitions, and eating fun stuff like roasted chestnuts and funnel cakes.

It was usually my favorite weekend of the year—USUALLY being the operative word in that statement.

This year from hell, instead of getting to hang out with my friends and ogle the out-of-town hotties, I had to stand on a street corner and hand out fliers and coupons from the various shops and restaurants on the main shopping drag in Old Town. IN THE MAN PANTS.

It blew. I probably didn't have to tell you that.

Here's what blew most of all: Dylan was excused from this particular exercise in humiliation, leaving me to toil in the misery alone. Yeah, again the FAIRNESS was in question.

The events stretched from the main drag in town to the Olympic launch ramp for the ski jumpers near the White Peaks ski resort, and DYLAN, as a member of the high school ski team (aka the ELITE), got to forgo Dacron polyester hell in order to don his tight-fitting hottie garb and perform exhibition jumps for the enthusiastic crowds. He had girls from a freakin' tri-state area fawning and swooning, whereas every guy alive was giving me and my large butt a wide berth, no pun intended.

The town looked perfect—all snow-covered and merry—and I didn't care. I glumly shoved fliers in people's hands, all the while hosting a gala pity party for myself.

I was down to a mere five MILLION or so fliers and

coupon books to hand out when Meryl and Caressa showed up.

"Hey, Lila." Caressa held out a hot cup of mulled cider, and the spicy tartness swirled up on the steam to tantalize my senses.

"Mmmm. Thanks." I gratefully set aside my stacks of handouts, hoping they'd all blow away, and took the cup. I watched my friends over the rim of my first sip. Mulled cider was just what I needed. I started to feel more positive. "What's up with you two?"

Caressa and Meryl exchanged a quick glance, then Meryl smiled at me bravely. "I've been researching new ways for us to figure out who our boyfriends might be. I think I found some stuff we can try."

My head was shaking NO even before she'd stopped talking. "Meryl, with all due respect, haven't we learned our lesson? The dumb supper resulted in nothing but disaster." I paused, indicating my outfit. "Why risk making things worse?"

"How could things possibly get worse?" Caressa asked. "I say, we try some of the ideas."

I scowled for a moment, but curiosity got the best of me. "Okay, like what?"

Meryl's face relaxed. She knew she had me. Reaching up to tuck her hair behind one ear, she said, "Well, one of the customs says to swallow the heart of a wild duck, and you can have whichever guy you want."

My eyes bugged. "Uh, ix-nay on the eart-hay. I'm not swallowing animal guts of any kind. I'll become a nun first."

Caressa laughed. "My reaction exactly."

"I know, guys. I wasn't going to suggest we do that. I just wanted to tell you the story because I found it interesting. Plus, it gives me comfort to know we aren't the most desperate girls in history."

"Good point." I sipped my cider, trying not to think of slimy duck parts. "What other ideas?"

Meryl gave us this evil grin. "Well, I read a thing where you cut your fingernails and grind the clippings into powder, then stir them into cider. If you give this concoction to your crush, he'll like you back."

I considered making Dylan guzzle my nasty fingernail clippings. The notion held some retaliatory appeal. "That cheers me up. But, what else?"

"A lot of ideas with apples."

"Huh?" Caressa said.

"Well, one tradition says that we should lick our knuckles and stick an apple seed on each one. Then someone else . . . like, for example, Caressa, you'll secretly name the seeds on Lila's hand. Once that's done, she'll wiggle her fingers until they all fall off but one. The one left is the guy she'll supposedly date."

"That sounds a lot better than swallowing animal organs. But then, what doesn't?" I mused. I glanced around the bustling marketplace. "If we're gonna do this, let's do it. Where can we get some apples?"

Meryl swung her backpack around in front of her, unzipped it, then extracted a plastic bag full of apple seeds. "I was hoping you were up for it, so I came prepared."

"Aren't you optimistic," Caressa said, with a laugh. She licked her knuckles and stuck out her right hand.

I pulled off my glove with my teeth and did the same.

Meryl carefully placed apple seeds on our knuckles, then licked the back of her right hand and extended it. I grabbed the bag of seeds and hooked her up.

"Okay, let's go around in a circle. Caressa, you name Lila's seeds, I'll name yours, and Lila, you name mine."

"Deal." We were all silent for a few moments, naming the designated person's seeds. I named the seed on the knuckle of Meryl's middle finger Ismet, for symbolic reasons.

"Ready?" Meryl asked.

I took a deep breath, released it, then nodded. We both glanced at Caressa.

"I'm ready," she said.

At the same time, we all started wiggling our fingers. I watched Meryl's hand, since I knew who her seeds represented. The pinky seed fell off first, then the index finger seed followed suit. Uh-oh. I started to get nervous. I stared at the seed on her flip-the-bird knuckle, willing it to drop off before the other one. Sure, the other one represented Peter Dickensheets, a computer-genius type from school with a name so profoundly WRONG, no one should ever consider marrying him. But I hadn't been able to think of anyone else on the spur of the moment. Besides, even a boy named PETER DICKENSHEETS was a better prospect for Meryl than a guy who didn't want her.

Alas, Dickensheets fell to the ground.

I stopped wiggling my fingers, unable to believe

that Ismet was the seed left, then I looked down and noticed that I only had one seed left, too. On my pinky knuckle. Caressa kept wiggling until only her ring finger knuckle still had a seed.

"Okay," Meryl said, breathlessly. She dipped her chin. "Who does my seed represent?"

I swallowed and thought about lying, but I couldn't. I blew out an annoyed breath. "Ismet."

Meryl looked startled. "Oh. Really?" I actually saw some hope blossom on her face, which sucked. I hated to see her get disappointed again.

I nodded. "What about me?" I asked Caressa.

"You don't want to know."

"Hutch?!" I rasped. "Don't tell me that's the freakin' Hutch seed, Caressa, or I'll know this was rigged."

She bit her bottom lip and nodded around a grimace. "It's Hutch. And how could it be rigged?"

She had a point. I flicked the seed off my hand.

We both turned our attention to Meryl. She'd gone so pale, her freckles stood out in sharp relief against her cheeks, and I dreaded hearing what she might say. Caressa extended her seed-endowed ring finger and arched a brow.

"Bobby Slade."

"What?" I shrieked. "Meryl, why did you even name a seed after him?"

"I had to!" Meryl spread her arms wide. "It wouldn't have been fair to Caressa if I'd left him off."

I groaned as I spun in a circle with my hands covering my face. When I opened my eyes again, I implored my brainy pal, "There has to be some mistake. Let's do something else."

Meryl tapped her bottom lip with the fingers of one hand. She stared off into the distance as if trying to thumb through the files of her mind and find just the right non-animal-gut-munching ritual.

"I kind of like how it turned out," Caressa said softly.

I pointed at her while staring at Meryl. "See? That right there is evidence we need to do something else."

Caressa smacked my upper arm with the back of her hand, just as Meryl said, "I know, I know. I'm thinking."

Finally, she nodded. "Here." Meryl handed us each two apple seeds. "Name one after"—she glanced around—"Hutch, and Caressa, you name one after Bobby. I'll name one after you-know-who."

"What do we name the second one?"

"Let's just call them nobody. Or if there is someone else you might like to date, name it after him."

Caressa looked at the first seed. "I deem you Bobby. And you"—she glanced down at the other seed—"you are hereby nobody. Now what?"

"Are you done, Lila?"

I peered cautiously down at the little brown seeds, named them in silence—Dylan and Brad Pitt—then nodded at my friend.

"Okay, close your eyes and stick one seed to each of your eyelids. On the count of three, we'll all open our eyes and start blinking. Whichever seed doesn't fall off—"

"We get the gist."

We spent a few minutes adhering the seeds to our eyelids with cider-scented spit, then Meryl said, "Ready?" We both said yes. "One, two, three."

My eyes flew open and I started blinking spasmodically, just like that one time a gnat had flown into my eye. My friends were doing the same thing. Before I knew it, we were all laughing like crackheads. I couldn't imagine what we looked like to the uninformed observer. Of course, I didn't have to.

"Well, well, well," came the snarky, fake voice of Hellspawn.

I spun and came face to face with Jennifer and her entourage of false blonde courage. I stopped blinking, but not soon enough.

The blondes snickered and shared evil glances.

"You have a bug on your eyelid, Lila," Hellspawn cooed. "But it probably fell out of your hair."

I blinked in surprise, and Brad Pitt fell off. SHIT!

"Why can't you guys be nice?" Meryl asked.

Hellspawn swept her with a derisive head-to-toe glance. "Why can't you be off my planet, freak?"

Caressa stepped forward, close enough that Jennifer had to look up to meet her gaze. It was an excellent study in intimidation, and I admired Caressa for it. "I have an idea. You get off our planet. We were here first."

A tense staredown ensued, but my buddy never so much as faltered. "God, Caressa," Jennifer said finally, stepping back. "You know, you could actually be cool if you didn't hang out with these losers."

"And you could actually be cool if . . ." Caressa frowned, sort of looking off to one side. "Hmmm. Actually, no. You couldn't ever be cool, Jennifer, because you're a raging bitch from hell, with a poorly done dye job to boot."

Hellspawn's thin-lipped mouth dropped open and she stared at Caressa incredulously. Her hand flew up to her dark roots, but she didn't seem really aware that the motion had given away her insecurities. Jennifer Hamilton wasn't used to those who she'd deemed to be lesser beings standing up to her, I supposed. Her face turned red and the big, thick vein in her neck pulsed with anger. Without another venomous word to us, she spun on her stiletto-heeled boots (totally wrong for the conditions) and snarled, "Come on," to her minions. They obeyed. NATCH.

After they'd huffed away, I grinned at Caressa. "Score one for the loser freaks," I said, with laughter in my voice.

"Yeah," Meryl said, high-fiving me and Caressa. "But forget them. The real question is"—she bit her lip, looking nervous—"which seed stuck?"

Oh. Yeah. That.

I stared at the street, sort of scuffing the toe of my boot against the gray snow. "Hutch," I said grudgingly.

"Bobby," said Caressa.

"Darn," said Meryl. "Mine didn't work right either." Always the optimist, she shrugged. "Well, look at the bright side. I guess it's good that we won't be dating *nobody*."

That's the whole point, Mer, I wanted to say. *We ARE and probably always WILL BE dating nobody. HELLO!*

Shefka and Jenita showed up a few minutes after the seed debacle, and the four of them traipsed off to visit some of the craft booths. I started handing people— especially children—WADS of the coupon books and fliers at a time, until finally I handed the entire stack to an infant in a stroller whose mother was peering into a shop window. I skulked off before she noticed her child was covered (harmlessly, I assure you) in coupons. I wanted to find my friends, but my feet started moving of their own volition toward the launch ramp at the individual normal hill, where the ski jump exhibitions were held. A new round was about to commence, and I told myself I was merely trying to be nice by supporting Dylan's efforts. Whatever.

I stood off to one side, out of the view of Hellspawn and her evil flying-monkey girls, who were preening and posing on the opposite side of the ramp. It was almost as if they weren't really there to watch Dylan and the other ski hotties, but rather so other people could SEE the hotties paying attention to them. Call me crazy, but that seemed convoluted—not to mention conceited.

I turned away from the blondes and tried to let myself enjoy being somewhere other than on a street corner foisting paper goods on strangers. A huge crowd had gathered to watch the jumpers, and after a few moments of focused positive thinking and deep breathing, I found myself caught up in the excitement.

Dylan competed both in ski jumping and Nordic combined for WPHS. The coach was grooming him to be the team captain next year, and there were even rumblings of Dylan and a couple other guys competing in the Olympic trials in a few years. That was mondo cool for Dylan, but how out of my realm would the guy be if he became an Olympic athlete? Then again, why was I even thinking that way? The guy was out of my realm NOW.

My enthusiasm dimmed a bit at the thought, but soon the first skier was positioned at the Inrun, and everyone began to clap and cheer. I shaded my eyes and squinted upward, trying to identify the skier, but it was hard. Moments thereafter, the announcer read off Dylan's name, and the countdown began.

My heart pounded with a combination of anticipation and fear. The individual normal hill was just under three hundred feet high. What if Dylan got hurt? What if he wiped out in front of everyone and his Olympic dreams fizzled? What if—

Dylan launched.

I held my breath as he flew down the ramp, covering my mouth when he hit the Takeoff. His form was freakin' awesome, though, and his landing was, indeed, Olympic-perfect. The crowd went absolutely wild, and I found myself clapping and sort of jumping up and down. I pushed my way toward the front of the throng, then stuck my pinkies in the corners of my mouth and let loose with a huge, long whistle. I glanced around at the rest of the spectators as they watched Dylan. The ubiquitous blondes were swooning and shrieking in his direction, hands outstretched. I blinked, and my smile faded.

I studied the faces of the other people pressed against the barriers around the landing area of the ramp. Just about every other one was that of a flushed, cute girl, going wild and screaming out Dylan's name. I wouldn't have been surprised if they'd started flinging G-strings and bras.

Who in the hell was I kidding?

Reality reared back and bitch-slapped me right across the kisser. Dylan Sebring was so completely NOT MY TYPE, and if this wasn't proof positive, I didn't know what WOULD be. The last thing I wanted was to be *one of many*, and looking around at all these starstruck faces, I knew that any one of these girls would do any-thing it took to have a boyfriend like Dylan—even screw over her supposedly best friends.

I wouldn't.

I stared down at the snow, which shimmered like a blanket of diamonds in the bright Colorado sun. God, what an idiot. I WAS one of the guys. But the big news was, that was perfectly fine, because I didn't want to BE one of the screaming girl masses, stomping over all the other girls in single-minded pursuit of the guy everyone wanted. I never wanted to BE that kind of female. Apple seeds were stupid. In fact, I would never consume another apple as long as I lived, just on principle. Ditto apple juice, applesauce, apple-flavored Jolly Ranchers. Maybe even Snapple.

My mood darkened, and I turned away. I might as well go find another narc and see what else needed to be done, because THIS was not my universe. All around me people continued to cheer and whistle and scream Dylan's name. I heard Hellspawn's voice clearly above the crowd.

"Dylan! That's my honey!"

HORK.

I tried to ignore her, but my eyes glanced over of their own volition. She had both cashmere-gloved hands cupped around her mouth and she was beckoning Dylan over. I looked from her to him and noticed he wasn't watching her, he was watching ME. My stomach jumped. Dylan waved vaguely at Jennifer, but skied over toward me. TOWARD ME! I wanted to walk away like it didn't matter, but I froze to the spot for a moment. I shook it off, with more than a little effort, and forced myself to take a step in the direction of sanity. But then—

"Lila! Wait up!"

GROAN. I turned back. A couple adults moved aside

and let me move to the front of the barrier. Dylan sprayed up a sheet of snow as he skied to a stop in front of me. He pushed up his goggles and smiled. "I didn't know you were into ski jumping."

"I—I'm not."

He winked. "Just wanted to watch me, huh?"

"Please." I rolled my eyes. "Don't make me puke on your skis. I was finished handing out fliers, so I just wandered over. There's nothing else to do."

"Yeah, sure. So . . . did you see my jump?"

Weird. He almost sounded vulnerable, as if he WANTED my feedback. But, how could that be? Didn't the throngs of screaming females give him a CLUE as to how his jump went over with the crowd? "Yeah, I saw it."

"And?"

My throat tightened. I thought about how amazing he'd looked, how confident and talented and sure of what he was doing. I remembered how I couldn't breathe while he was winging down the ramp at warp eighty, and how exhilarated I felt when his jump turned out perfectly. Luckily, I verbalized none of this. In fact, I managed to just shrug. "Well, you stuck the landing."

Dylan laughed and shook his head. "Always Lila. That's one thing I can say about you."

I scoffed. "Brilliant observation, not that I'd expect anything profound from a jock."

He grinned. "So, how's it going?"

"It sucks. Duh."

He leaned in. "Miss me?"

My heart stopped. Why was he affecting me like this? It pissed me off. I was practically turning into a Jennifer clone, except for the being-a-giant-bitch part. "Dream on, Sebring. If I missed you I'd take a deep, calming breath and re-aim."

He really laughed at that one. "Man, how do you always know the right thing to say?"

GLUG. "Whatever. I gotta go."

"Okay." He settled his goggles back into place. I was glad, because I didn't have to look into his eyes anymore. Then again, the goggles-on look cast all the focus onto his lips. ACK. "Thanks for coming to watch me."

"Sure," I said, as if doing so had been an afterthought.

"I'll see you later, Lila. I know, I know, not if you see me first." Dylan skied away, and for a moment I felt glum. Then I caught a glimpse of Hellspawn's furious, disbelieving expression and realized two things:

(1) I'd succeeded at making her writhe with jealousy once again, and (2) Dylan had ignored her and skied toward ME. He'd CHOSEN to speak to me rather than her, and he'd done it all in front of her and a zillion other people, including the evil flying-monkey posse.

My mood brightened immeasurably, and I tossed her a taunting little waggle-fingered wave. Forget finding another narc. I'd worked enough for one day. I headed off, instead, to find my friends and tell them what had happened. Apple seeds were still the enemy, but I had to look on the bright side. Hellspawn's day was ruined, and surely Meryl would have another, preferably seedless, idea for finding our destined boyfriends.

I loved making Jennifer Hamilton squirm with jealousy, no doubt, but I was jacking with my own mind as well. A dose of reality was in order. Nothing good would come of my stupid crush, hence I HAD to get Dylan off my mind. At this point, I was up for just about anything.

Well . . . other than swallowing a wild duck heart.

BLECH!

eleven

* * * * * * * * *

meryl

I finished dusting off the front display shelves at Inner Power, then stowed the cleaning supplies in their little cabinet underneath the front counter. After that, I went from section to section blowing out candles and incense, and turning on the lamps that were to be left lit while the store was closed.

I loved my job, and I loved my bosses. Kelly hadn't worked that day, but Reese was in the back room tallying up the day's sales, which had to be great since we were so close to Christmas. I know we had more foot traffic that evening than I'd seen in a long time, and I'd rung up an amazing number of purchases. I was exhausted, but in a good way.

As I walked the floor completing my closing duties,

I pretended I was one of the owners of the funky little metaphysical shop rather than a part-time clerk. How cool would it be to own a business like this? I would wear long flowing outfits every day and a signature armful of tinkly bangle bracelets. My entire aura would exude serenity and confidence at all times. People would flock to me and ask my advice about everything from Wicca to weddings to *which guy to date.*

If only.

Over the past month, Lila, Caressa, and I had made full use of Inner Power's resources on our quest to find the perfect guys, but it had never worked out. No matter what we tried, fate kept stubbornly pointing us back to Ismet, Dylan, and Bobby. So, as far as the whole shop-owner fantasy went, believe me, NO ONE should ask my advice on who to date . . . or even how to find out!

But, it didn't matter, because I wasn't one of the shop owners. Unfortunately, I *was* only the part-time clerk, and even more unfortunately, I had places to go and lots of things to do before I could hit the sack that night, so my delusions of grandeur had to stop.

The rhythmic *click, click, click, whirrrrrr . . . click, click, click, whirrrrrr* of the adding machine carried through the otherwise silent store, and I hated to interrupt Reese while she worked. But, I only had a small chunk of leeway time between when I left Inner Power and when I needed to show my face at home to avoid questions. Plus, our tiny Sears store didn't stay open too late on weeknights. I had to get there at least half an hour before they closed if I wanted it to be worth my while.

None of this had ever been a problem for me before.

Don't think about it. You don't have a choice.

With a deep, calming breath, I leaned my head inside the door to the tiny, brightly lit office and pasted on a smile. "Excuse me, Reese?" I said softly.

She glanced up, a pleasant expression on her makeup-free face. She kept one finger pressed onto the stack of receipts so she didn't lose her place in the adding, I assumed. "All done out there?"

"Yeah. I'm going to take off, if that's okay."

"You have a lot of studying to do before finals?"

Something like that. I averted my gaze and felt instantly crappy about the fact that I had been lying to basically everyone in my world since the White Peaks Christmas Market. Even Lila and Caressa. Even *myself*, if I really thought about it—which I tried not to. You know what they say . . . *denial* is more than just a river in Egypt. "Uh, yeah."

"Well, you'll do great, as always. But if you need to cut down on hours or study at the cash wrap desk when business is slow, that's fine."

"Okay. I appreciate it."

"You go on, Meryl. See you this weekend. And thank you."

"You're welcome. Bye," I said, feeling a fresh stab of guilt. If I was falling behind on my studying, it sure as heck wasn't because I'd been working too much.

I slipped out the front door of the shop, relocking it behind me, then hunched my shoulders against the cold, ominous wind. I pulled my collar up around my cheeks and prayed I wouldn't run into anyone I knew. Once I'd made it safely inside my Volvo, I breathed a sigh of relief and mentally sketched out my evening. I would head to Sears, put in another session of Operation: CIA (Catch Ismet's Attention), and rush home in time to relax and spend time with my family.

I was basically leading a double life, but I couldn't see any other way to solve my ongoing guy problems. I mean, COME ON. The dumb supper and the two separate apple seed experiments came up with the same result: Ismet. Subsequent tarot and rune readings and other little rituals confirmed the fact that Ismet was allegedly the guy for me. All that repitition had to mean *something* significant. And yet the only way to snare him was to somehow transform into a cool, all-American, pop-culture-savvy teenager. It was a NIGHTMARE, because I felt completely out of my element.

Hopefully, though, not for long.

Nightmare or not, I wanted Ismet Hadziahmetovic to see me as more than a dorky little school pal, so I was doing what I needed to do to make it happen. If it meant I had to sneak around a little bit, compromise my convictions temporarily, well, it sucked but I hadn't been able to think of a better way. I knew Lila and Caressa had become underwhelmed about my chances with him, but if it was just a matter of a little television . . .

I parked sort of behind Sears near the Dumpsters, just in case one of my friends drove by and caught a glimpse of the car. My Volvo was totally recognizable and I'd be so busted. I'd hate that, because—truth told—I wasn't 100 percent comfortable with, nor was I 100 percent proud of, these clandestine nights spent at Sears.

I slipped into the store as I'd done so many nights before and, head down, I wound through the aisles I'd come to know by rote until I reached the TV section in the far corner. With a sigh, I pulled the program guide I'd smuggled along out of my backpack and gave it a quick scan. There was this show about winning a million bucks that sounded vaguely intriguing. I didn't know what the show was, but I mean, who *doesn't* want to win a bunch of money? Duh.

I walked up to the TV in the farthest back corner and pushed buttons around until I happened upon the channel I needed, then I sat back and watched. My attention kept drifting, but the money show seemed to be some sort of televised testing process, where participants were awarded dollar amounts for answering the test questions correctly, and they lost money for giving the wrong answers. However, I couldn't tell if the money they earned was symbolic, like Monopoly money, or real. No bills ever exchanged hands, let me put it that way.

Huh.

It wasn't that I *hated* the show, or any of the shows I'd been exposed to since I'd begun sneaking into Sears to watch TV, but the underlying point of them was lost on me. I certainly couldn't fathom how watching this or any of the shows would make a girl more dateworthy.

Still, I kept watching, hoping I'd get the point.

Operation: CIA, and all that.

I answered all the questions correctly on the money show, which was at least fun, if not surprising. But aside from that, I just had to ponder the question of WHY I would want to watch some stranger being tested on their knowledge in order to win money. Why would anyone? Once, maybe. Or if you knew the person on the show. But, otherwise, it kind of annoyed me.

Then again, maybe I just had to reframe it in my mind. I mean, it *was* kind of like debate, only glitzier and more cheesy. Maybe I could get used to it . . . but the thought of that made me feel bleak and grumpy. The whole bottom line was, I sort of wished Ismet would like me for ME, and not for my knowledge of television and stuff. Because I sure wouldn't mind having my normal life back, only with Ismet as a part of it.

I'd been disturbed to realize that my eyes had been more tired at night after I'd spent an hour or two staring at the Sears televisions, and I'd even started getting headaches. Not to mention, I had developed an almost constant nervous stomach, because I felt like I wasn't being authentically me.

Part of me felt like what I was doing was wrong.

The other part of me just wanted Ismet to LIKE me.

And there I was, stuck in the middle and feeling yanked by both sides. Tears stung my eyes, and I sat down cross-legged on the floor, leaning my back against a shiny chrome dishwasher. (The store was really small, so display space was at a premium.) I watched a bit more of the money-winning show, then crawled up to the television and hit channels until I got to this show where people who thought they were ugly got made over by experts and plastic surgeons and stuff. Again, explain to me why watching this would make me a catch?

"You can use the remote, you know."

I scrambled to my feet and spun toward the voice, my heart pounding in my chest. The statement had come from a thin, late-twenties-looking guy wearing dress slacks, a short-sleeved white shirt, and a shiny electric blue tie that sort of didn't go with the outfit. He had a Sears employee nametag pinned to his pocket, and he lounged against the chrome dishwasher with one ankle hooked over the other, just kind of studying me.

My throat tightened. "I'm sorry?"

"The remote."

I had no freakin' clue what he was talking about, and it must've showed on my face.

"To change the channels, you know? You can use the remote." He waited for the big A-HA to register in my eyes, and when it didn't, he picked up a little calculator-looking thing and showed it to me. "Instead of going up to the television, you just point this." He demonstrated, taking us back to the money show.

"Oh. You mean . . . from across the—oh yeah." I touched my forehead. "That's right. I forgot."

He laughed. "Where exactly do you come from? A little house on a prairie somewhere?"

Embarrassment flushed through my body in a hot sweep, but I lifted my chin. "I just don't have a television, is all. I didn't remember the dumb"—I flicked a hand—"remote control." Sheesh. How hard is it to get up and walk to the TV, anyway?

He stopped teasing and cocked his head to one side. "You don't own a TV at all?"

"No."

"Did you ever?"

"Nope."

"What about at friends' houses?"

I shook my head.

"Wow, trippy."

"Look, I've *seen* remotes. I mean, I'm no idiot, but I just . . . never mind." I wasn't going to explain the lifestyle quirks of my family to the Sears appliance guy, for God's sake.

He pushed up off the dishwasher and walked a few steps closer. "Is that why you're here several nights a week? Deciding on a television to buy for your folks, perhaps?"

Man, I hadn't thought about the possibility of someone noticing the weird redhead loitering in the home entertainment department on a regular basis. Was I in trouble? I mean, loitering was a crime, right? I stalled, tucking my hair behind my ears. "I'm just . . . checking them out. Sort of."

"Where do you live?"

I had immediate flashes of the Sears Police driving me home, lights and sirens ablaze, and telling my parents what I'd been up to. It's not like they'd kill me or anything, but I would hate to disappoint them or make them think I didn't like our life the way it was. Then again, Sears didn't have its own police force as far as I knew, so I was probably wigging for nothing. Still, I took a hesitant step back and flicked a glance around. "Why?"

He held up both palms. "Relax, I'm just curious. I have a friend who subsistence farms at about ten thousand feet of elevation. He doesn't have electricity, running water, or any of that. Hence, no television." He shrugged. "I guess I just wondered if that was your deal."

Now I looked like a subsistence farmer?! God, no wonder no one wanted to date me. I started to feel irritated by the conversation, even though he seemed nonjudgmental and basically harmless. Still. I stooped over and grabbed my backpack, then slung it over my shoulder. I tossed my hair and leveled a hard look at him. "No, I live in a regular house with flush toilets and everything," I said sharply. "We just don't have a TV. It's not a required household item in America, you know."

He pulled his chin back with what looked like surprise. "Look, I didn't mean to pry and I certainly wasn't passing judgment. I don't watch much TV myself."

I glanced away, shamefaced. Why was I so defensive?

"Anyway, you seriously don't have to leave." He spread his arm toward the wall of blathering boxes. "Feel free to watch as long as you like. I won't bother you."

"No. I—it's okay," I muttered. "I need to get home anyway." I spun toward the front of the store and started walking swiftly down the polished, white linoleum floor. My arms were stiff at my sides, my hands in tight little fists. Suddenly, I started to feel like a jerk for my snotty behavior, and I turned back. The Sears guy didn't deserve to be on the receiving end of my Operation: CIA frustration. I met his gaze directly, even though it wasn't easy to do. "Thank you. For talking."

"What's your name?"

Should I lie? Then again, wasn't I doing enough of that these days? Without warning, I felt really tired. I just didn't want to add another layer to my web of deception. "Meryl."

"Named after Ms. Streep, I assume?"

"Who?"

He chuckled. "Never mind. I'm Mike, and you're welcome. For the talking, that is. I meant what I said." He tilted his head toward the bank of televisions. "You can come in and catch a show whenever you want."

What if I don't want to, but I feel like I have to if I ever want a date? I bit my bottom lip and seriously thought about asking him, but at the last minute I decided it wasn't his problem. I gave Mike, the Sears guy, a closed-mouth smile instead. "Okay. Thanks."

Caressa

Another New Year's Eve had come and gone, and none of our rituals had succeeded in pointing us AWAY from Dylan, Ismet, and Bobby. After the apple seed rituals at the WP Christmas Market, we'd tried everything else we could think of. We'd had our tarot cards and runes read at Inner Power. We took a Saturday drive to the Metaphysical Fair in Denver and had our palms and tea leaves read. We tried scrying, Wiccan love spells—I even dropped a hundred bucks calling a 1-900-psychic, not that I'd admit it to my friends. But, anyway, NOTHING we tried gave us direction on how to fix our lives, and everything pointed to the three guys who hadn't worked out whatsoever.

Well . . . not *yet*. At least in my case.

It was already the week of Valentine's Day, and I'd convinced myself that Bobby Slade hadn't written back to me because he'd been out on the road. But I happened to know that his twenty-second birthday was February 14. (Google is a beautiful thing.) Surely, he'd be home celebrating the big two-two with his family. Here's what I figured: Bobby would take a birthday break from touring, and while spending time at his home in Louisiana, he'd take a few moments to catch up on all his correspondence, which included getting in touch with me.

Voilà! Perfectly logical.

That line of reasoning is why I found myself sitting by the front window watching for the mail carrier like a dog with a fondness for biting. Don't ask me how, but I just *knew* there would be something from Bobby Slade. I don't CARE about Lila's and Meryl's skepticism—fate was sending me a loud and clear message: Bobby Slade was my destiny.

As I waited for the mail, I killed time by painting each of my toenails a different color from OPI's Greek collection, looking up every few strokes to be sure I didn't miss our rural carrier, Roland. Mail delivery was different up here in the mountains. There were a few of the standard red, white, and blue mail trucks people are used to seeing, but they usually made the rounds right in the center of town. For the outlying neighborhoods, most of the mountain post offices contracted carriers. In plain English that meant regular folks delivered mail to us right out of the windows of their personal vehicles. Cool, huh?

Our mail carrier, Roland, is a nice old toothless guy who drives an orange Volkswagen Thing, which is this übercool ugly car from the olden days. He's really friendly and carries milk bones for all the dogs who live on his route. I don't think any of them have ever bitten him. He's too nice! Plus, he wears regular clothes instead of that oh-so-recognizable uniform that makes dogs go, well, postal.

Just then, I saw the Thing bounce up the dirt road and creak to a stop at our mailbox. I scrambled to my feet and waddled toward the front door as fast as my foam toe spacers allowed. I had bought a special pair of open-toed slippers, with thick rubber soles and felt uppers that closed over the top of my foot with Velcro but wouldn't mess up my pedicure, and I hurriedly put them on. Dad must've heard the commotion, because he appeared at the door of his study, holding a music book and peering at me over the top of his half-glasses. He always looked ancient when he did that.

"Hi, Daddy."

"Where's the fire, young lady?"

"I'm just going out for the mail."

"Hmm." He leaned one shoulder against the jamb and studied me with those creepily all-knowing paternal eyes. They made me feel transparent. "Expecting anything in particular?"

Ummmmm . . . uh-oh. Hadn't seen that one coming. I cleared my throat, searching my brain for an answer that would seem feasible. Birthday cards . . . nope. Not my birthday. Bills? Nah. I don't have any. Presents—that's it! Gifts to myself, that is. "Oh, just a shipment from Sephora.com." I smiled blandly.

Dad stared at me for a few moments, then shook his head and sighed. "What could you possibly need from them, child? Between you and your mother, we own every cosmetic known to man right here in this house."

I rolled my eyes. "Very funny, Daddy."

"Well, hurry on back in, *chérie*. It's cold out there. I don't want you to catch your death."

"Okay." I reached for the door handle, but my dad stopped me before I could get outside.

"Oh, Caressa. Tell me something."

I gave him a put-upon sigh. "What?"

He tipped his head to the side and removed his glasses, tapping one earpiece against his bottom lip. "Doesn't UPS usually bring those boxes from Sephora.com, rather than the U.S. Postal Service?"

WHOOOOOOOOOOOOOOPS. He was right. Who knew the old guy paid that much attention?

I laughed nervously, but managed to cover pretty well, I thought. "Oh. You're right. Huh. Oh well, I'll just run and get the mail anyway."

"Mm-hmm," Dad said, before raising his eyebrows in this certain disconcerting way, then slipping back into his study.

Okay, he was giving me the willies. Did he know something I didn't? Or did he suspect something that wasn't true? Or something that *was* true, which would be infinitely worse. Or had he somehow intercepted a reply from Bobby Slade written to me?

Waitonefreakinminute!

I screeched to a halt right there in the portico, realizing the gravity of my mistake. My obvious, horrible, I-shoulda-known-it-from-the-beginning mistake. HOLY, HOLY, HOLY CRAP.

BIG DUH—any reply from Bobby would've come addressed to my DAD, not to me. The forged letter looked, obviously, as if my dad had written it. It was SUPPOSED to look that way. WHY HADN'T I CONSIDERED THIS BEFORE? I WROTE the stupid thing, and yet, in my lovesick haze, this had never occurred to me.

AUGH!

There went any career aspirations as a spy.

Then again, if my dad had already received a reply from Bobby Slade, wouldn't he have mentioned it? I mean, it would've baffled him, since he'd never WRITTEN a letter, so he would have started poking around to get to the bottom of it . . . right? I was almost sure he would have, but I certainly couldn't get all Nancy Drew about it now. If I started asking questions, odds are my whole forgery ploy would be exposed and I'd be grounded for the rest of my life. I wouldn't be able to hang with LILA anymore, that's for sure. My parents would start thinking she was this big criminal influence, which is SO undeserved. I probably wouldn't be getting any more prize packages from Sephora.com, either. URK.

God, I'd dug myself a Lila-esque hole with this one.

I hurried to the mailbox and found, of course, nothing of interest inside it. Back in the house, I kicked off my pedicure slippers, tossed the mail on the entry table, peeled out my foam toe spacers, then took the stairs two at a time until I reached my room. Forget the pedicure. I'd fix it later.

I signed online and checked for Meryl and Lila. Meryl wasn't on (where WAS she these days?), but Lila was. That worked, because she was my partner in crime anyway. I IMed her.

Lipstickgrrrrl:

Lila! :-O Help!

LawBreakR:

What??

Lipstickgrrrrl:

I royally screwed up!!!!!

LawBreakR:

How? What? What's going on?

Lipstickgrrrrl:

U know the letter 2 Bobby?

LawBreakR:

Um . . . DUHHH!! I signed the thing, remember?

Lipstickgrrrrl:

I never considered the fact that, SHOULD Bobby reply, it would go 2 MY FATHER, not 2 me.

LawBreakR:

:-O

LawBreakR:

Oh crap! R U telling me your dad got a letter from Bobby Slade? R U totally busted??

Lipstickgrrrrl:

No, I don't know if he got a letter at all. But, short of going through my dad's mail, which I simply won't do, how will I ever know?

LawBreakR:

[sigh] Settle down, Caressa, ya freakin' crack smoker. Think about it logically. If your father got a letter or phone call back from Bobby Slade, he'd put 2 and 2 2gether and your a** would be grass. DON'T BORROW TROUBLE (as my father says). U haven't heard anything because Bobby Slade hasn't written back. CHILLLLLLLLL-LLLL.

Lipstickgrrrrl:

U really think so? [fret]

LawBreakR:

I know so. Come on, have I ever steered U wrong?

Lipstickgrrrrl:

ROFLMAO!!!!!!!!!! Only like every freakin' day of my life since 5th grade, U dork.

LawBreakR:

Ha ha, you're so funny—NOT. :-) Don't worry. 4GET about Bobby, and I mean it. (Please, GOD, 4get about Bobby.)

Lipstickgrrrrl:

I wish I could. [sigh]

LawBreakR:

That makes 2 of us. I gotta blaze, girl. I'll TTYL, okay? Keep me posted. [SWAK]

Lipstickgrrrrl:

Okay, thanks. Where R U headed?

LawBreakR:

Some stupid junior narc thing. What else??

Lila—unfairly persecuted and deprived of a life.

Lipstickgrrrrl:

LOL. TTYL, GF. Kiss Hutch 4 me.

LawBreakR:

GAK—shut up.

I signed off and decided to make a conscious decision to chill. Lila was right. I was most likely worrying for nothing. Bobby Slade would be in touch as soon as the time thing worked out for HIM. I released the stress of it, but I *did* plan on going through the mail just a little bit more thoroughly from here on out. If I did see a letter to my dad from Bobby Slade, I'd clip it before it ever landed on his desk.

I flung myself on my bed and closed my eyes with a pleasant sigh. Hey, I could afford to relax. Bobby and I had the rest of our lives to spend together, after all. Why rush things?

twelve

It was March. ALREADY. I could hardly believe it. My life was completely passing me by, kicking my butt and taking absolutely no prisoners. T-minus two months and counting until prom, and my buds and I remained woefully "dateless in da mountains." We didn't even have real prospects—some things never change!

It had been an überbusy, draining winter for all of us, and, looking back, it seemed like junior year was a steep mountain we were all sliding down, unable to grasp a single fingerhold. I SO didn't want to hit the bottom. Life had turned into one big out-of-body experience, and OHMIGOD, we were going to be seniors in, like, five and a half months. DATELESS seniors, if we didn't do something drastic, and quickly.

Wanna know the worst part? As Meryl's, Caressa's, and my school and extracurricular commitments had revved up over the year, we'd started to see each other less frequently. SUPER BUMMER. We all felt SO out of touch. I don't know if our dads had planned it that way, but it sure felt like an evil paternal plot to keep us apart so we didn't get into any more trouble.

Meryl had been working a lot and studying like a mad fiend—even more than she usually did. It seemed like Caressa and I hardly ever saw her except (1) at school, and (2) online (occasionally). I mean, she was ALWAYS off studying, which was weird, even for her. If you want my opinion I think she was studying too hard, because she seemed a little bit down whenever we talked. I have to say, I missed my bubbly Meryl buddy who could find a bright side of anything—even the vomitous man pants.

As for my universe, I had been putting in a ridiculously unfair number of hours with the narcs. I was now certified in first aid and CPR. Yeah, I know, yipp-freakin'-ee. The weird thing was, as much as I still despised being sentenced to the group, I had begun to let myself secretly enjoy spending time with Dylan. I hated to admit it, but he was cooler than I'd ever imagined he would be, what with all the major strikes against him at first glance.

He and Jennifer had broken up and gotten back together so many times since the Christmas Market, everyone had started to call them J-Lo and Bennifer. It was a giant eye-roller, their so-called relationship. I had high hopes that he'd eventually come to his senses and dump her altogether, but so far, no luck.

Pros? I got to hear the dish about their relationship straight from Dylan, and it made me realize how NOT to act with a guy, if I ever scored one. Jennifer's main complaints about Dylan were:

(1) He spent too much time on junior narc stuff (true)

(2) He spent too much time with MOI (not true at all)

(3) He didn't give her enough attention (but who could? she was high maintenance to the core), and here was the best one:

(4) He didn't appreciate what he HAD in a girl like her (ummm, I'll bite. A relationship not unlike a hemorrhoid?)

Cons? It completely blew to be crushing on a guy who was taken, even in their on-again, off-again way.

Especially in their on-again, off-again way. I mean, he'd choose to be with a psychowench like Jennifer instead of a cool chick (like me)?

SIGH.

Dylan knew of Jennifer's hatred for me, but the awesome part was, he didn't let that affect the way we related or worked together. A more irritating guy would totally kowtow to his girlfriend's insecurities and treat other girls badly just so his arm shrew didn't freak. Dylan didn't. Big points for him.

DOUBLE SIGH.

I'm sure he surmised that the negative feelings were mutual, though I never uttered an ill word against Jennifer in front of him. But, as much as he spilled his guts to me about dwelling in dysfunction junction, I noticed he never asked my advice about what to do with their whole train wreck of a relationship (which was wise, since my advice would be KICK HER TO THE CURB, DUDE). I really liked that he felt he could come to me whenever he needed to vent, though. It got to the point where I KNEW he was talking to me more than he was talking to her. I guess I'd put that into the PRO column, too.

On Planet Caressa, the theatrical nightmare was finally coming to an end. It had been a long haul, but *Beauty and the Beast* was opening tomorrow night! She was in the throes of a major dread fest, but the rest of us couldn't wait. Hey, reluctant or not, Caressa was a pro. Her apathy about playing Belle wouldn't prevent her from putting on her game face tomorrow in order to rock the house. Meryl and I had tickets for the premiere, and we planned to go early and snare the front row seats. I could only hope the expected spring snowstorm wouldn't postpone the play.

So, basically, my friends and I had slipped from hopeful dumb supper attendees into major woe-is-us mode. As I've learned, though, life just has this way of keeping things in perspective. Whenever things get really bad, fate tends to step in and remind you that your problems aren't that huge in the scheme of things.

That's how it was that Thursday.

It was a GOOD Thursday in a lot of ways. There was no school thanks to a teacher planning day. I had no narc obligations, always a blessing. And the impending storm meant there might be some upcoming snow days, which were really hard to come by up here in the mountains.

A lot of my friends had hit the slopes that morning, but I was feeling mopey, and I wasn't up for getting caught in the storm. I'd been in Colorado spring blizzards before—no thanks. Trust me, they made you FORGET it was almost summer, even though we almost always had our biggest snows in March and April.

Anyway, the mopey part came into play because Dylan and Hellspawn had recently gotten back together after split number one zillion, and it just seemed unfair. Meryl was scheduled to work at Inner Power all day, and Caressa was tied up with final dress rehearsals. I decided to hide out at home and work on a paper for English. I had put it off way too long, thanks to the giant time-suck that was junior narcdom.

I'd claimed the dining room table as my study area, so I could spread everything out. It was two in the afternoon. I'd been toiling away with my research for a couple hours when my dad walked in.

"Hi, *m'ija*." He crossed the room and kissed me on the top of my head, then laid a hand on my shoulder.

"Hey. How come you're home so early?"

"Things were slow. I came home to make sure we're all stocked and ready in case this storm is a big one."

"Is it supposed to be?"

"Hard to say, but it pays to be prepared." He crossed the room and grabbed an apple out of the bowl on the sideboard, then came back and leaned over my notebook. "Whatcha working on?"

"An English paper that's practically late because I'm always stuck doing stupid narc stuff," I said pointedly.

"Oh, come on. You seem to be really enjoying it lately."

"HA. And I thought they called cops trained observers. Newsflash, pops, I DESPISE being a narc. Always have, always will." I never missed an opportunity to vent my displeasure over the punishment thing.

He just ignored me. "So, how's the paper coming?"

I sighed at his lack of compassion for my plight, but then again, I was used to it. "I don't know. It's fine, I guess."

The legs of the chair scraped on the floor as Dad pulled it out and took a seat perpendicular to mine. "Can you take a break for a moment?"

"Sure." I laid my pen down. "What's up?"

Dad studied my face for several seconds, then smiled. His eyes shone warmly. "I'm proud of you, Lila."

Huh? Had my dad been rockin' the confiscated ganja

from the evidence lockers at the station? "Are you feeling okay?"

"No, really. I am proud of you." He reached over and smoothed my hair. "I know you didn't want to join the Police Explorers, my dear daughter, and that you take every opportunity to express how much you despise it. But you've adapted really well. You're a lot like your mother in that way. She could protest louder than any woman I'd ever known, but she always put her heart and soul into everything."

A warmness radiated through my stomach. I loved knowing I was like Mom, but not in relation to the narcs. Please, God. I struggled to maintain my poker face. The praise felt good, but I couldn't afford to make Dad think I actually APPRECIATED being a narc in any way, shape, or form. I was determined that the hell would end when the school year did. I quirked one eyebrow up and took a slow, unconcerned sip of my Pepsi, hoping the nonchalant move would properly convey my indifference.

Dad went on, oblivious to the subliminals. "And you know, Dylan tells me you're doing a great job with the crew, and that you take direction well and you're always cooperative and pleasant to work with."

My unexpected burst of laughter caused a stream of fizzy Pepsi to shoot out of my nostrils and spray all over my notes. It hurt. I launched into a near-death coughing bout, banging the side of my fist against my upper chest and wondering if anyone had ever died from pneumonia contracted after having aspirated a carbonated soft drink. Dad, meanwhile, mopped up the nostril spray with a paper towel.

He whipped a worried glance at me. "Are you okay?"

I nodded, but my eyes were watering like crazy and my throat was sore. "Went down the wrong tube," I explained, in a wheezy voice. When I could speak without feeling the shards-of-glass-through-the-chest-wall pain I simply had to confirm what I'd heard. "Dylan said all that about me?"

"He sure did."

Man, just another example of why Hellspawn Hamilton didn't deserve the guy. Here I'd thought Dylan would yessir and nosir himself to death in the presence of the almighty Chief Moreno, but I'd been wrong-o, in a gigungous way. I was humbled to know Dylan hadn't ratted me out as the surly, insubordinate, unmotivated problem-child that I was. "Huh. I wonder why."

Dad looked amused, but curious, too. "You disagree with what he said?"

Yeah, like I'd do that. NOT. I shook my head no.

Dad laughed. "Okay, enough grilling and praising. Go back to your paper, Lila Jane. I just wanted to make you aware of the fact that I've noticed and I'm pleased with the changes I've seen in you so far."

I flashed him a hopeful half-smile. "Can I quit the narcs early then?"

"Nope."

"Well, can I at least have a car?" Couldn't hurt to ask, what with the parental love fest going on.

Dad stood and gave me a wry wink. "Don't push your luck."

What the heck good did the praise do me if it didn't result in the reinstatement of lost privileges? "But, Dad—"

"Talk to me next year, Lila."

"Next YEAR?!"

He held up a finger. "Stop right there. You've modified your behavior, and that's a good thing—"

"Well, then—"

"Now I want to see if you can make it stick."

"It will!"

"We'll see. Then, and only then, we'll discuss cars."

"But—"

"No buts." He pointed at the table. "Write." And, with that lovely little bit of news, he left the kitchen. ARGH!

I was still pouting over the no car until next year edict when I heard the doorbell ring, but I didn't jump up. What was I, the house lackey? I didn't care who might be there anyway. I couldn't concentrate on my paper, so I sat there thinking about (1) my lack of wheels, (2) Dylan and his heinous girlfriend, and (3) neverending narcdom, all while doodling little cubes and stars in the margins of my notes. I tried not to stew too much about any of it, but it was hard not to.

After a few moments, Dad stuck his head into the dining room. "Lila? You have company."

I swiveled my head around to look at him. "Who?"

Dylan popped up behind my dad. "Hi."

Dylan?!

I jumped up from my seat and smoothed my clothing, hoping I didn't look like too much of a slob. Then again, what did I care? Dylan liked his women blonde and bitchy. "Oh. Hi."

Dad, thankfully, gave Dylan one jovial guy slap on the back, said good-bye, then slipped away. As annoyed as I was with him about the car thing, I had to give the old man props for not standing around listening to our conversation, rendering my life more hellish than it already was.

The question remained, why the heck was Dylan here?

"I didn't realize you'd be studying today. Can you talk?" he asked, glancing down at my papers.

Only then did I notice his face looked strained, and his usually perfectly messy hair looked messier than usual. It bordered on the not-cool, which I found so totally cool. GOD, the guy was annoyingly yummy. "Um, yeah. Sure." I hesitated, uncertain what to do next. I mean, we talked at school sometimes, and at the junior narc trainings, meetings, and events. But he'd never come over to my house.

I moistened my suddenly parched lips and flicked my hand sort of helplessly at the fridge. "Want something to drink?"

"Sure. Pepsi?"

I nodded, stupidly giddy to learn that he was a Pepsi guy rather than a Coke guy. I crossed to the fridge and extracted two cans of Pepsi. I didn't want to drink my old one in case some of the nostril spray had gotten in it. As an afterthought, I snapped up a bag of chips, too.

It felt too weird being in the house, despite the fact that it was getting colder outside. Luke or my dad might walk in at any time. Blech. Turning, I tilted my head toward the back door, then pointed at my North Face ski jacket hanging on a hook. "Grab that for me. I'll show you my favorite rock."

That was one cool thing about living in the mountains. We didn't have to set up fake cool areas to sit outside . . . like patios or gazebos or whatever. I mean, they were fine, but we had naturally cool areas, courtesy of Mother Nature herself. Our land was flat in spots, steep in others. We had pine trees, wild-rose bushes, an aspen grove, and best of all we had huge rock outcroppings that had served as perfect thinking and/or brother escape places over the years.

I led Dylan across our property without talking until we reached my favorite boulder. Suddenly, I felt shy and sort of dorky. I shrugged. "So, anyway. This is where I come when I need to get away from my dad and brothers for a sanity break."

Dylan flashed a small, wry smile. "You basically live out here then?"

My anxiousness eased some, and I smiled back. "How'd you guess?" I took a seat, then handed him a Pepsi.

It was weird, but I hadn't slipped into rebellious Lila mode, and I didn't really want to. Maybe it was because we weren't doing some narc activity, but I had a sneaking suspicion that it was more because I'd gotten to know Dylan over the months, and he seemed more human and normal to me than I'd ever imagined he would.

An icy wind kicked me into shiver mode, and I thought maybe I should've suggested hot chocolate instead of cold pop. Too late now. I took my jacket from Dylan and put it on, set the chips between us, then asked, "So. What brings you over to my house for the first time ever?"

"I was here before."

"When?"

"The night your dad sent me to get you at Caressa's."

I rolled my eyes. "For the love of God, Sebring, don't bring *that* up. I was totally on a not-hating-you kick for a few seconds there, and you ruined it."

He didn't smile like he usually did when I snarked on him. Instead, he sat, and his shoulders drooped slightly.

"What's wrong?"

After releasing a long sigh, he popped his Pepsi top, but he didn't drink. "Jennifer and I broke up."

"Again?"

"For good this time." He peered up at me from beneath his lashes. "I'm serious."

I have to say, it was an act of pure will and an amazing feat of brilliance that my facial expression didn't change, because my entire mind, body, and soul were doing the major happy dance at the news. But, I was shocked to realize that one part of me felt really sorry for him. I'd begun to think of him as a friend, I guess, and it always blew to see a friend suffering. "What a drag, Dylan," I said softly.

"Not really," he said, which both surprised me and made me happy. Not to mention curious. "I mean, the breaking-up part sucked, but we haven't been getting along for a while now, as you well know." He flashed me a sidelong glance. "I hope you don't mind me coming over here to dump this on you."

I hiked one shoulder. Was he high? I loved that he turned to me before anyone else. "What are friends for?"

He smiled then, so sweetly that it made my stomach tighten. "Most girls wouldn't say that, you know."

"I'm not most girls."

"I know." He paused for a long time, then reached over and drew some design on my knee with his finger.

I nearly died.

"Sometimes it feels like you're the only person I can really talk to."

A warm flash of pleasure moved through me, but I forced myself to remember I was ONE OF THE GUYS. I didn't want to get my hopes up, just because Dylan was here.

"Which is another reason I came over—"

Before Dylan could finish his sentence, Dad slammed his way out of the house, pulling our attention away from the conversation. He glanced around until he saw us, then lifted a hand to beckon me. I sighed and stood. "Hold that thought. I'll be right back."

I trotted over to Dad, who was looking very serious. A little alarm bell sounded inside my head. "What's wrong?"

"I'm heading to the PD. We have a hiker lost somewhere near Elk Bugle trail."

Uh-oh. I glanced out toward the mountain range that cupped our neighborhood, noting the ominous, slate gray clouds rolling in. On the verge of a heinous spring storm was definitely the WRONG time to get lost in the mountains. "Okay. Be careful."

He glanced over my shoulder toward Dylan. "If the storm hits, I want Dylan to head home right away."

"Okay."

"Before the roads get bad, Lila. I mean it. Unless he's comfortable getting snowed in at our house."

GLURK! My face flamed like I'd stuck it over a Bunsen burner and held it there. "Uh, yeah. That's not going to happen, Dad."

"Good." Dad glanced at his watch. "I'll check in as soon as I can. Be good."

" 'Kay. You, too."

Dad chucked my chin, then headed off in his company 4x4.

I jogged back over to Dylan, who looked totally curious.

"What's up?" he asked.

"I guess there's a hiker lost near Elk Bugle trail."

I could almost see Dylan's ears perk. "Really? We may get called out to help with the search."

My heart actually jumped with excitement. Search and rescue sounded like a much cooler detail than tearing tickets. "I didn't know we did stuff like that."

Dylan rolled his eyes. "That's because you see exactly what you want to see when it comes to the Explorers, Lila, and most of it's bad."

"Whatever."

We didn't even have a chance to get back to the meat of our previous conversation before Dylan's cell phone rang a few minutes later. He pulled it off his belt clip and checked the caller ID. "The PD," he told me in a worried voice, before flipping the face open and answering. "This is Dylan." A pause. I stared at his profile, trying to get a feel for the conversation. "Hi, Chief."

My dad?

"Uh-huh. Uh-huh." All of a sudden Dylan's expression changed from psyched to scared. "Oh no."

Prickles of fear seeped into my mind, so I looked away and thought about song lyrics. Obviously something terrible had happened, but I'd get the 411 soon enough. Why rush it? I looked up into the graying sky just as the first, fat snowflakes began to fall, and MAN, did that feel like a foreboding sign.

After a moment, Dylan said good-bye, snapped his phone shut, and stood. "Come on. We have to change into our uniforms and head out."

"Where?"

"To the command post at the Elk Bugle trailhead. Your dad is launching a major search due to the snow. We won't have much time if it really starts coming down." He pointed at his car. "I have a uniform in my gear bag. Can I come in and change?"

"Of course." For once, I didn't even pout about having to don the polyester nightmare. I jumped to my feet as well, snatching up the potato chip bag. As we rushed over toward Dylan's car, I asked, "Do they know who the hiker is?"

"I guess it's actually a child who wandered off alone." His gaze locked with mine, and I got a huge honkin' case of goosebumps. Both of us knew this could be really, really bad.

I just had no idea HOW bad. At least, not right at that moment . . .

thirteen

*░░ ░░░ ░░░ ░

The command post buzzed with a sense of urgency when we got there, but an unspoken undercurrent of doom kept things subdued. The snow had begun falling sideways—a BAD sign. All of us knew that blizzard snow fell sideways. About fifty search and rescue people had already gathered, with more expected. I glanced around at my fellow narcs and everyone else, and read the fear on everybody's faces; I absorbed the feeling of tension and the itch to get moving.

One of the cops was busy handing out bright orange vests, headlamps, flares, and other safety equipment to all of us, and a second officer was taking names and assigning numbers to each team of two. Dylan and I were assigned to work together, and I was glad. He'd done backcountry search and rescue before. Sure, he wasn't a trained member of Alpine Search and Rescue, but I knew Dylan and felt comfortable with him. I trusted him more than I realized I ever would.

While the equipment distribution was underway, my dad stood up front with a megaphone and laid out the search plan for all of us. The white glare of the ambulance lights, which had parked behind the mobile command post vehicle, illuminated him. It seemed like a scene out of a suspense flick.

In a calm and reassuring voice, my dad gave out pertinent information and went over the rules for the safe search. I have to admit, apprehension and adrenaline kept me from hearing much of what he said. But, as I watched my dad take control of this very scary situation, I couldn't help but admire his confident and cool collectedness. I mean, all of us were feeling uncertain and terrified of what we might find—I could feel it in the air like an electrical crackle just before a lightning strike. But Dad made us all feel like we were charged with the most important job ever, and he had faith we would carry it out capably. Simply through the words he chose and the way he spoke, he imbued the entire crowd with confidence to match his own.

I glanced around and saw that every volunteer out there, as well as all the cops, firefighters, and other rescue personnel, was gaining courage from my dad's laid-back but in-control leadership. It struck me, at that split second, why my dad was so admired and respected in White Peaks. Freaky. I saw him, maybe for the very first time, as the large-and-in-charge professional that made my brothers, and so many other guys, want to be just like him. At that moment, *I* even wanted to be like him.

The shocking revelation made me tune Dad out completely. I just had to wallow in my unexpected wave of respect for him. It was a full-on feelin'-the-Moreno-family-love moment, and it totally floored me.

"Oh, crap."

Dylan's exclamation startled me, and I blinked my way back into the present moment. "What's wrong?" I whispered. His face had gone sort of white and pinched.

He pointed toward my dad. "Didn't you hear what he just—"

"Lila!"

I spun away from Dylan at the sound of Meryl's urgent voice. My confusion grew. What was she doing here? Wasn't she supposed to be at work? Had the news of the missing child traveled through White Peaks so quickly that the town closed down business for the day? I mean, Meryl wouldn't have heard about it on television.

As she jogged toward me and Dylan, her red hair flew out behind her. Ismet and Shefka jogged only a few steps behind Meryl, which surprised me anew, and all three of them looked panicked. I started to freak, so I ran over to meet them.

When Meryl got close enough, I saw that her face was streaked with tears. I grabbed her upper arms to brace her. "What's wrong?"

"It's Jenita."

"What?"

"The lost child. It's Jenita Hadziahmetovic," she said, with a catch in her voice.

"Holy—" My stomach plunged. "What happened?"

"She and my parents were up here before the snow, and she wandered off," added Shefka, who had just caught up and was out of breath and wild-eyed. "She is always in her own world. I cannot imagine what made her . . ." Shefka burst into tears, stifling her sobs with a fist against her mouth. Ismet maintained his composure, but he put his arm around Shefka and pulled her close.

"We have to find her"—Ismet said what we were all thinking but afraid to say—"before the snow gets worse." He tipped his head back and stared at the sky, blinking as the flakes landed on his eyelashes.

We all followed his gaze, and none of us were happy with what we saw. The snow was coming faster and harder. We had a small window of time in which to turn this situation from a tragedy to a miracle.

"We want to join the search," Meryl said, in a determined tone. "Who do we talk to?"

"I-I don't know, Mer." I whipped a glance toward my dad. He was busy, so I beckoned Dylan over. When he reached us, I simply said, "It's Jenita."

"I know. That's what your dad told the group."

And what I hadn't heard. I wondered what else I might have missed while I'd been lost in my own thoughts.

Dylan addressed Ismet and Shefka. "Don't worry, you guys. We *will* find her."

"In time," I added firmly, before turning to Dylan. "Meryl, Ismet, and Shefka are going to join our team." I didn't ask, because there wasn't a chance in hell I'd tell them they *couldn't* assist in the search, even if he balked. Sure, none of them had training, but let's face it, neither did I. Not for this. Besides, if I had a little sister who'd gotten lost in the mountains during a snowstorm, nothing would stop me from doing all I could to find her, including lack of training.

Luckily, Dylan didn't argue at all. He pressed his lips together and nodded once, looking grim. "Let's get them vests and lights then. We need to get going."

Search and rescue, I quickly learned, was a painstaking process of moving slowly in a pattern through the search area, all while calling out for the lost person and making sure every square inch of ground was checked in case she was hurt or unconscious and unable to reply.

Horrific thought.

Initially, the five of us stuck together, but pretty soon we decided we'd cover more ground quicker if we spread out.

Meryl, Shefka, and Ismet split off, and Dylan and I stayed together. We were careful to remain within yelling distance of each other, though, and we checked in every minute or so.

The snow came steadily harder, and each time I looked at the sky, panic welled up in my throat. I managed to hold it back and continue the search, but when I pictured Mr. and Mrs. Hadziahmetovic back at the command post fearing the worst, another wave would hit. I did my best to push away the terror and forge ahead, because I knew the only way out of this nightmare was to find Jenita safe and sound. But I'd never been so scared in my life. The upside was, I had never felt so focused before, either. We absolutely *would* find Jenita, because the alternative was too awful to contemplate.

For the first time ever, I felt grateful and sort of empowered to be a part of the Police Explorers, even to be wearing the uniform. I drew comfort from the ugly thing. Wearing it meant I didn't have to stand by helplessly. I could actually do something constructive. I felt proud that I could make a difference, no matter how small, with something this important. In contrast to the ticket ripping and other stupid tasks, I wanted to give my all to this process, and then some.

It wasn't about the uniform.

It wasn't about my punishment.

For the first time in a long time, it wasn't about ME.

I wanted to use every skill I'd learned, and most shocking of all, I wanted people to look at me when this was all over and think, *Hey, that Lila sure is her father's daughter.* This moment was real life, and I was a Police Explorer with an important life-or-death role. I didn't feel like a fraud. Instead, I felt like a lifeline to little Jenita.

Premature darkness had fallen, and about five inches of snow had accumulated by the time we found her.

It happened like this:

Dylan and I had been calling out for her, checking every bush and gully and ravine with no luck. Two hours or so into the search, we came upon a big pile of boulders. Dylan scrambled to the top. "Jenita!" he called out, just like he'd done a hundred times before. But this time . . .

"I am here," I heard, coming from somewhere to my left.

My heart crashed against my ribs and my skin began to tingle. My entire body trembled. "Dylan! I heard her."

He spun back to face me. "Where?"

The sheer urgency made me shake my hands as if I'd burned them and bounce up and down. "I don't know. Call her again!"

He cupped his hands around his mouth. "Jenita!"

"Here," came her weak reply.

Dylan and I both moved toward the general direction of her voice, then we froze and listened. "Jenita, keep talking to me."

"Help me."

We ran closer. Dylan made his way down the boulders and grabbed my hand. Both of us were shaking. We held on tight and listened with every bit of our attention.

"Are you okay, Jenita?" Dylan called out.

"No."

We exchanged a frightened glance.

"Stay where you are and keep talking," Dylan instructed. Despite the physical evidence of his fear, his voice remained soothing and strong. "What's wrong with you? Why aren't you okay?"

"My ankle is hurt," she said, her tiny voice going a bit wobbly. "I fell."

"Oh no," I whispered to Dylan.

He put his arm around me and pulled me against him briefly. "It's okay. We found her and it's just her ankle. She'll be fine."

I choked back the urge to cry and nodded.

"Jenita!"

"I am here," she called back, and it sounded like we were right on top of her.

Both of us whipped frantic glances all around us.

"By the tree."

Of course, there were trees everywhere, but it helped that she was speaking to us. We needed to follow our ears and hold back our panic, and this nightmare could end.

"Tell me if we sound closer, Jenita!" Dylan hollered, moving toward his left.

"Here!" Her voice sounded more excited. "Over here!"

Dylan and I both scanned the area, and my eyes settled on something pink. A pair of pants. "Look!" I pointed.

There was little Jenita, down at the bottom of a ravine, sitting against some exposed tree roots. She was protected, somewhat, from the weather, but woefully underdressed for the storm. Her teeth chattered, and snow had begun to pile up on her outstretched legs. Just seeing her like that made my world swirl down to a wavery black pinpoint of nausea. I closed my eyes and breathed deeply until the urge to faint passed.

Still, we'd found her. The knowledge of how much worse this could've been kicked me in the gut. If we had not walked in this direction and happened upon her, she never would've been able to survive the cold weather. And she couldn't walk out, because she'd hurt her ankle.

GOD, the worst-case-scenario images sickened me.

We slipped and scrambled our way down to her, and only when we were at the base of the small ravine with her did I catch sight of her ankle, twisted unnaturally to the side. My stomach rolled, and I bent forward to put my head between my knees. *Deep breaths. Don't puke.* I took a moment to mentally cross ER doc off my list of possible career choices. Ditto paramedic and nurse, or ANYTHING medical at all.

Dylan, thankfully, wasn't similarly woozed out. "Hey, Jenita," he said, in this comforting voice that completely contrasted with the fear sluicing through my veins. "Don't you worry, we're going to take you back and get you some help, okay? How's that ankle?"

Jenita had been holding it together, but at the sound of Dylan's voice, she started to cry. "It hurts."

Dylan squatted down and ruffled her hair ever so gently. "I know it does, kiddo. But we're here now, okay? You did a great job helping us find you."

"I want my mom," she wailed.

Dylan turned to me, and I knew what he was thinking without either of us saying a word. We couldn't give Jenita her mother, but her brother and sister would be a good alternative until we got her down the hill to safety.

"Call for the others," he said in a low voice.

I nodded, then scrambled my way out of the ravine. I cupped my tingling hands around my mouth. "Meryl! Ismet!"

"Over here!" came Ismet's reply.

"We found her!"

"Where are you?"

It was so stormy dark, and I didn't know how to best describe my whereabouts. After a moment, I pulled the mini Maglite off my equipment belt and flashed a strobe of light onto the top of the boulder Dylan had climbed when we first heard Jenita. "Do you see my light?"

"Yes!"

"Walk toward that boulder and turn right. You'll see me."

After more back-and-forth talking and continuous strobing with my beam, all three of them came crashing through the woods in my direction. I waved my hands wildly.

"Is she okay?" Ismet called.

"She broke her ankle, but otherwise she's fine, I think."

"Thank goodness," Shefka said, breaking down into tears again. "Thank goodness for that."

When we were all together, I led them swiftly back to Dylan, who was completely focused on the little girl as we approached. His calm command of the situation amazed and impressed me. In the short time I'd been away, Dylan had somehow managed to get Jenita smiling. He had removed his coat and wrapped her in it, and his ski cap was on her little head. He must have been freezing, but if so, he didn't show it. A gush of affection filled my heart as I watched his sweet, gentle manner with her. Meryl must've felt it, too, because she reached over and squeezed my hand.

Ismet and Shefka rushed to their little sister's side and started speaking to her in soothing tones. I didn't know what they were saying, because they were both speaking Bosnian, which seemed to calm her. Jenita cried when she first saw her siblings, but they appeared to be tears of relief rather than fear.

Dylan stood, lobbing me his radio. "Call down to the command post and let them know we found her, okay?"

GLURK! "Okay. W-what should I tell them?"

He gave me an encouraging smile. "That she's cold and has a fractured ankle, but other than that it's all good news."

I nodded, but I felt out of my element. I took a moment to plan out a very professional radio transmission. I decided it would go something like, "Team 33 to the command post, we've located the party. She has a fractured ankle and cold exposure, but she's fine otherwise. We're en route to your location."

My heart was nearly thrumming out of my chest at the prospect of what I had to do. I know it seems stupid, but I'd never talked on the radio before and the whole freakin' department, not to mention all the volunteers, would be listening. I whispered a quick prayer, keyed the mike, then said, "Team 33 to the command post." I unkeyed and waited for acknowledgment.

"Team 33, go."

It was my dad.

Unexpected tears clogged in my throat. Relief and fear and a whole tangle of emotions overwhelmed me, and my little copspeak speech went straight out the window. With sobs in my throat, all I could manage was, "Daddy, it's Lila. We found her."

We were greeted at the command post like heroes, surrounded by applause, cheers, and whistles of joy. News media had gathered, and the whole area was brightly lit by spotlights on the various pieces of emergency equipment and news vans packed into the trailhead parking lot.

The paramedics took over care of Jenita the moment we broke out of the trees—thankfully, because the hike down had been painstaking, exhausting, and stressful. Tears filled my eyes as I watched Jenita's parents weeping with relief and raining kisses on their little daughter's face.

Everyone was hugging and crying and laughing all at once, and I stood back with a huge grin on my face and took it all in. We had averted something horrible, and we knew it. Suddenly, one of the cops grabbed me and gave me a giant hug. After I'd been passed around for congratulations to what felt like hundreds of cops, volunteers, and friends, my gaze locked with Dylan's across the crowd. We grinned at each other, and it felt like everyone else disappeared. It seemed like slow motion when he started walking toward me but finally he threw his arms around me, picked me up, and twirled me around.

I laughed, but when he set me down, he didn't let go. The mood of the moment changed and my throat went dry.

"Thank you," I whispered to him.

"For what?"

"For making it less scary."

He pulled back. "Don't be silly, Lila. You did amazingly well up there."

"Well, I didn't puke," I conceded. "But, I couldn't have done any of this without your help."

"And I couldn't have done it without yours," he countered. "So, how about if you let me thank you by taking you out to Mountain Lion Coffee for a cappuccino."

My heart jumped, and I swallowed hard. I so so SO wanted to go. "B-but the snow is getting so—"

"Come on, Lila. It's practically on the way home."

"You two should go on," said my father, who'd approached without me noticing. "You did a great job up there, *m'ija*. Go relax and have some fun."

I threw my arms around my dad's neck, surprising him, I think. He stiffened for a split second before wrapping me in a giant bear hug.

"I love you, Daddy."

"I love you, too, Lila Jane, and I'm so proud of you." He pulled back, then planted a smooch on my cheek. "Go have a cappuccino, then head home. I'll be there later."

I looked from him to Dylan, who was watching me with hope and expectation in his eyes.

"Okay." I smiled. "Let's go."

fourteen

* ■ ■ * ■ ■ * ■ *

Outside, the snowstorm raged, but the interior of the Mountain Lion coffee shop welcomed us with warm gold lighting, soft alternative rock music from a Boulder station, and the delicious aroma of freshly ground Jamaican beans. Bright orange flames licked and crackled inside the fireplace, and I spied an unoccupied sofa in front of it.

Me. Dylan. A fire.

How much did this rock the my world?

A multipierced college student with excellent dreadlocks sat studying at one of the tables, but other than her and the barrista, the coffee shop was empty. The walls, painted warm mango, seemed to embrace us. In fact, sitting inside Mountain Lion Coffee, you'd never know that a major tragedy had just been thwarted on the Elk Bugle trail. Being in the little coffee shop made my whole soul sigh with relief. Being there *with Dylan* had the same effect on my heart.

I felt both exhilarated and exhausted by what we'd gone through. In fact, I felt permanently changed in a lot of subtle ways. The most interesting switch had happened inside my head, though. I hadn't seen it coming, but all of a sudden, I had no interest in being my regular snarky self with Dylan. I wasn't even so invested in hiding my crush anymore.

I wanted to ask him questions, to find out more about who he really was. I wanted to find out what had prompted him to join the junior narcs, because the more I got to know him, the less he seemed to resemble my brother, Luke. (Bonus!)

Dylan Sebring piqued my curiosity. He made me want to know everything there was to know about him, about myself when I was with him . . . even about the potential of an US.

YIKES!

"Grab a table," Dylan said, looking around. "I'll get us a couple cappuccinos."

"Can I have a caramel machiatto instead?"

He grinned. "That's a total chick drink, Lila."

"So? I happen to be a chick, you know."

"Don't I know it," he said ruefully.

I punched him in the *Where the Wild Things Are* tattoo spot, wondering what he meant by that. "I thought you said I was like one of the guys? If you're going to insult me, you can't say I'm one of the guys AND a total chick. Pick one or the other."

"Lila, you *are* like one of the guys, but I meant it as a compliment."

Inside me something fluttered. "Oh."

"Duh," he said, in this sarcastic tone that made me want to hug him. He made a face at me and headed up toward the counter.

Feeling a million kinds of warm and fuzzy from our snitty banter, I eschewed the idea of a table and made a bold move: I went for the cozy loveseat by the hearth instead. Screw it. If the dumb supper and a million other ridiculous rituals were going to point me in Dylan's direction, I was going to take advantage of this non-date-esque date to find out WHY.

I stopped in front of the loveseat and shrugged out

of my feloniously ugly parka, then sank into the cushy pillows. The snow outside the big picture window looked magical from where I sat, and the firelight and warmth felt magical on my skin, too. I couldn't think of anywhere I'd rather be than right there with Dylan. I *could* think of a few outfits I'd rather be wearing for this particularly romantic moment, but man pants or not, I wasn't going to knock spontaneity.

A couple of minutes later, Dylan approached carrying two coffee drinks in thick, plum-colored mugs, and a couple of white chocolate cranberry biscotti, too. My stomach growled, and I realized with a jolt that I was freakin' starving.

"It's been a long time since we've eaten," I said.

"Hungry?" He set everything down on the little table in front of the loveseat.

"Way," I told him. "You?"

One side of his mouth quirked up as he removed his jacket. "So, let me get this straight. You'd actually eat in front of me?"

I gave him the "what are you, a freakin' lunatic?" look. "Well, uh, yeah? What kind of question is that?"

"I don't think I ever saw Jennifer eat," he said.

My gut tightened. "Yeah, well, I'm not Hellsp— I mean, Jennifer."

"Don't I know it."

Another "don't I know it." Now I had to sit back and wonder what he meant by THAT, too.

He plopped down on the loveseat next to me, then leaned forward and grabbed the mugs. Handing me one, he winked and said, "Cheers."

I pushed aside all my wondering. "Yum. Thanks." We clanked mugs and sipped. I wrapped my hands around both sides of the warm ceramic and inhaled the heavenly aroma. Sometimes the smell of coffee was even yummier and more comforting than the taste of it.

Dylan blew out a breath and rubbed his forehead. For the first time, I noticed that he looked tired.

"Wiped?"

"A little," he admitted. "You?"

"Totally."

"Your dad really rocks in that kind of an emergency, Lila."

"Yeah." I sighed, feeling a little stab of guilt wrapped up in a whole lot of respect. "I hadn't really taken the time to notice that about him before, but today he made me proud to be his daughter."

Dylan's eyes were warm, intense. "I have a sneaking suspicion that you made him proud to be your dad, too."

My tummy did that flippy thing again, and I bought some composure time by sipping my coffee and taking a bite of the crunchy biscotti. "You know," I told him finally, "you're a whole lot different from how I expected you to be when this whole, hellish junior narc nightmare began."

He chuckled. "How did you expect me to be?"

I made a *gag me* face. "You know . . . like a typical jock. Like my brother, Luke."

"Come on. Luke's a good guy."

"Spare me."

"He is."

"He used to be." It made me sad. "Until he hooked up with Miffany."

"Well," Dylan conceded, "Miffany's definitely a hag."

I raised my mug. "Finally, an assessment we can agree on."

He lifted his mug, too.

We sipped, then I asked, "But, if you think Miffany's

vomitous, why date her best friend? Haven't you heard that you can tell a lot about a person by looking at their friends?"

"Yeah, I know. I don't know how to answer that, though." He cleared his throat. "But, what I really want to know is, what am I like?"

"I don't know. Kind of . . . normal."

He laughed. "And that's a good thing?"

I shrugged. "Yeah." I took another sip, and then I remembered my dad's big speech in the dining room earlier that afternoon. The whole conversation seemed like it had happened weeks ago, but I totally owed Dylan. "By the way, thanks for telling my dad I was doing a good job with the narcs. I never thought you'd lie on my behalf, but that was cool of you."

"I didn't lie."

I pulled my chin back with skepticism. "Oh, come on. You told him I was pleasant to work with, for God's sake. Unless you're a chronic glue sniffer, you can't possibly believe that."

He nodded. "Yes, I can. I happen to think you're a blast to work with."

"I complain constantly."

He inclined his yead. "You protest a lot, but you do good work while you squawk, Lila, and you're funny."

I sat back and studied his face for a few moments. He seemed sincere, and I realized I needed to know more about this guy, right here and now. "Tell me something."

"Snow is cold."

"Shut up, Dylan."

He grinned. "Okay, what?"

"How did you get involved with the narcs?"

It was his turn to lean back and study me. "How do you think I did?"

I reached up and scratched my cheek while I considered it. "I don't know. I guess I thought you dug the idea of being in authority, so you joined up the moment you were allowed to. Like all the Moreno men. You know, the whole gung ho, macho jock thing."

Dylan's expression remained amused.

"What?"

"You're so judgmental, Lila Jane."

I narrowed my gaze into a threatening scowl. "Call me that again, and you're a dead man. Besides, I am not judgmental! I call 'em as I've always seen 'em."

"Hmmm."

"So? Are you going to tell me?"

"What?"

"How you came to be a junior narc."

"Oh, that." He sipped, then swallowed. "I stole a car."

My brain froze. "Huh?!"

He flipped his hand. "Well, not 'stole,' technically. At least that wasn't my intent. I took it for a joyride on a dare. Summer before last."

I could not believe what I was hearing.

"Some old friends of mine and I saw this amazing car parked over by the north boat launch at the lake. It was a Viper, unlocked, with the keys in the ignition."

"Tempting."

"Way. We started joking around, daring each other to get inside and take it for a spin. You know how ninth grade guys are."

I made a BLECH face. "Unfortunately."

"I wasn't planning on getting in, but they challenged me one time too many and I couldn't resist."

I scoffed. "See? Typical jock."

"Be quiet." He reached across the cushions and plinked my forehead with his finger.

"Ow!" I rubbed the stinging spot, but even the plink gave me tummy swirls. Man, I was in trouble with this guy. Especially knowing he was more hottie-rebel than I'd ever given him credit for!

"Anyway, I decided just to take the Viper for a short spin and return it to the exact spot where we'd found it, unscathed. Unfortunately, the White Peaks PD had other ideas."

"They ruin all the fun."

"Yeah." He huffed out this humorless little laugh. "The owner of the car, I guess, saw me drive off in his ride. He called 9-1-1, and they snagged me in a matter of minutes."

"Score one for the good guys."

"I guess." He looked chagrined. "I got pulled over and arrested less than a mile from where I'd snatched the car."

Wow. I mean . . . wow. "Dude, can I say that completely doesn't seem like something you'd do? Not even under the influence of testosterone overload and peer pressure."

"I know. And, I'm not bragging about the car thing." He ruffled his hand through his hair. "I was at a really low point in my life, I guess. It was just after my parents divorced, and they were *not* getting along. I felt like each of them was trying to use me to hurt the other one."

"That blows."

"Yeah. We've made up, though." He leaned against the arm of the loveseat with his back and propped one leg up on the cushion between us. I could feel his body heat from the nearness of that leg, and I liked it.

"But, still. The car theft isn't my proudest moment." He seemed to struggle with his next words. "Your dad really saved me, though."

I blinked at him in confusion. "My dad?"

"Yeah. I was all set to go on probation and even do a little bit of time in juvenile hall, if the judge decided to make an example out of me. Your dad pulled rank, called in favors, whatever. I'm not sure how it all came about, but the next thing I knew, I found myself sitting in his office. He told me that I needed to be a part of something that would teach me discipline and respect for the rules."

Ha! It was the same spiel Dad had laid on me. I smirked. "Did you think he was going to enroll you in karate?"

"What?" Dylan looked lost.

Hmmm. Maybe the karate thing really had been a mental stretch. Who knew? "Never mind. Go on."

Dylan shook his head, as though to rid it of cobwebs. "When your dad gave me the chance to prove myself with the Explorers, I couldn't jump on it fast enough. I mean, it was that or juvie and probation."

"Not much of a choice."

"No. And even though your dad knew exactly why I was in the Explorers, he never treated me like I was some dirtbag delinquent who needed to be closely monitored." Dylan gave a self-derisive snort. "I know how rebellious I was back then, and that wouldn't have worked for me at all. Instead, he gave me responsibilities and encouraged me to study for and take the promotional tests. It was as if he believed in me."

"He probably did."

"Yeah, but he had no reason to. See what I mean?" Dylan shook his head slowly. "I know you think being an Explorer is the worst thing in the world, but it saved my life, Lila. My parents were so caught up in their own trauma back then, and I'd started hanging out with some real slackers. I don't know where my head was."

I swallowed tightly, my respect for Dylan blooming into something huge and leaving me breathless. "Thanks," I said. "For telling me all that."

He shrugged. "In answer to your unspoken question, yeah, I wanted to be like your dad. I still do. But that doesn't mean I want to become a police chief."

"No?"

He shook his head and grinned. "I want to go to the Olympics. But no matter what career I choose, I want to be the kind of *man* your dad is." He flipped his hand. "I mean, he gives people the benefit of the doubt, even when they might not deserve it. He looks past the behavior and sees the potential, and *that* is what he focuses on."

It was true. I just hadn't seen it so clearly.

"I want to always remember that people make mistakes. I want to give them choices and chances. Pay it forward, you know? I owe him that much."

That sense of pride in my father returned sharply. My dad had played a key role in transforming my number-one crush into the awesome guy he was. It had a freaky kind of karmic justice to it. I admitted to myself that, in the past, I had made a few snap judgments. Maybe my fear and loathing of being a junior narc was one example. (Although the man pants were still ugly, and nothing would change my opinion on that.)

I finished my machiatto and set the mug on the table. "So, do you like being an Explorer, or do you like the fact that it saved you from juvie?"

"Both. At first it was just an easy ticket out, but the more I participated, the more I respected myself. And the more I respected myself, the better I felt about my parents' divorce, my life, my future—all of it." He cast me a playful sidelong glance. "It's fun being an Explorer. Plus, it helped me to stop making knee-jerk assessments about other people."

I knew he was nudging me, much like my father had probably nudged him back then, to do the same. "Give me an example."

He pursed his lips and thought about it. "Okay. I used to think girls like Jennifer were the ultimate prize. Who wouldn't want to date them, you know?"

UGH. I hadn't expected that. Jealousy hauled off and kicked me square in the gut. "Oh."

"But now, I've had the chance to meet a more unique girl."

My heart revved. "You have?"

"Yep. She follows her own path and doesn't fall into that annoying clique behavior. She'll eat in front of me. Plus she's funny and smart and witty and beautiful and well, not very nice."

I blurted a nervous little laugh. "Who?"

"You."

GLURK! Was this actually happening? I wished I could digitally record this entire moment, so I could play it back at any speed, zoom in, zoom out, and all that stuff at will. "Me?"

"Yup." He reached across the back of the sofa and gently brushed tendrils of my hair away from my neck. "I've never known anyone like you, Lila."

"W-what do you mean?"

"With other girls, I always felt like I had to play the role of the popular jock. As if they liked my image rather than the real me. That's a lot of pressure. Besides, I don't feel like that guy deep inside."

"Yeah?"

"Totally. But see, I don't feel that pressure from you."

"That's because popular jocks are usually major tools."

He laughed and tugged at my hair a little harder. "See? With you, I can just be myself." His expression grew serious, and his voice got huskier. "I like it, Lila. A lot."

AHHHHH, he was leaning closer! I felt like a tornado was touching down inside my stomach, so I went for the flippant reply. "It's nice to know you have the capacity for taste in women, Dylan. I was really beginning to worry about you."

He grinned. "Lila?"

"What?"

"I so totally want to kiss you right now."

ACCCCCCCCCCCCCCCCCCCCCCCK!!!

"Y-you do?"

"Yep. How do you feel about that?"

I moistened my lips with a quick flick of my tongue. "I feel like I'd rather do it than talk about it."

Dylan released a low, totally hot little growly laugh, then leaned forward. He cupped my cheek gently, and his eyes locked with mine. "I've wanted to do this for the longest time."

"Y-you have?"

"Oh yeah. Want to know something?"

"Um . . . sure."

"Jennifer was jealous of you."

I snorted. "Not a newsflash, Sebring. Tell me something I didn't know."

"Alright. She had every reason to be jealous of you."

My heart absolutely soared. He almost didn't have to kiss me for that moment to be perfect, except he went ahead and did it, and the moment transformed into freakin' stupendously, life-altering perfect. His lips were warm, soft and firm at the same time. It was the best first kiss in the history of the universe, and I made a mental note to send Jennifer a thank you note for giving Dylan the practice.

Ha! Not really, but the thought cheered me so much that I decided this day, which had started out so badly, had turned out to be the best day of my life.

Dylan pulled back from the kiss slightly. "Lila?" I could feel his warm breath against my mouth.

"Yeah?"

"Do you want to go out?"

My stomach quivered with excitement. "You mean, 'go out,' go out?"

He laughed softly. "Yeah."

I smiled. "Okay. On one condition."

Dylan laughed again, all private and intimate-like. "Why doesn't it surprise me that you have conditions?"

"Do you want to hear it or not?"

"Whip it on me."

I reached up and traced the edge of his jaw with my finger. I only wondered if that was a stupid move for a split second, and then decided it felt just right. "I'll go out with you, if you promise that one of our dates is to prom."

He pulled his chin back. "That's it?"

"What do you mean, that's it?"

"I was planning to ask you a long time ago, but I needed to get things with Jennifer squared away and make sure you didn't totally despise me first."

"Are you serious?"

"Dead."

I could have killed him. If he only knew the trauma I'd gone through trying to get fate to point me AWAY from Someone Else's Guy. But I had to forgive him, because, hey, we were going to prom!!! At least, I thought so. He hadn't actually confirmed it. "Are we going to prom together, then?"

"We're going to prom together."

I grinned. "That totally rocks."

"I'll say." And then he leaned in and kissed me some more.

We were so caught up in each other, in sharing little coffee-flavored kisses, that it took three rings before we noticed that someone was calling Dylan's cell. He pulled away from me, yanked his phone off his belt clip, then read the caller ID. His baffled gaze flicked up and met mine. "It's Caressa."

"Huh? Why's she calling your cell?"

"I don't know." He flipped it open. "Hello?" A pause ensued, while he listened. "Yeah, hi. She's right here."

I cocked my head questioningly, and he shrugged and handed the phone over.

"Hey, Caressa."

"Lila." Her voice was more wigged than I'd ever heard it before. "Holy, holy, holy crap. I'm so glad I found you."

I sat forward, immediately alarmed. "What's wrong?"

"Nothing. Or maybe everything," she rasped. "I'm not sure at this point because I can't think straight."

"What's going on?!" I demanded.

"He's here."

"Who?"

"Bobby Slade. He's at my house."

"NO WAY!"

"Way. Freakin' totally WAY. He's in my dad's studio as we speak, jamming the blues with my father."

fifteen

* ■ ■ * ■ ■ * ■ ■ *

meryl

Svuda podji svojoj kuci dodji.

That was a Bosnian phrase I'd learned that meant, "You can travel the world round, but you will always return home." I hadn't realized how utterly true it was until that day.

In the aftermath of the crisis, Ismet's mom rode along to the hospital in the ambulance and his dad followed behind in the car. I offered to drive Ismet and Shefka there, but they wanted to go home instead, to get things ready for Jenita's return. That meant making up her bed with clean, soft sheets, putting fresh flowers we'd picked up at the grocery store in a vase on her nightstand, and cooking her favorite Bosnian dish—a really yummy-smelling spiral pastry and meat thing called *burek*. I was honored when they asked me if I'd like to help.

Exhausted as we all were from the search efforts and stress, bustling around the house getting things in order gave us a sense of purpose. Soon, however, we'd finished. Jenita and Mr. and Mrs. Hadziahmetovic had returned home, with Jenita's broken ankle trussed up in a bright pink cast. The entire family hovered around, showering her with love and tenderness. I welcomed Jenita home, too, but soon I started feeling out of place and awkward. I hung back, but soon even that wasn't enough. There is a time for friends and a time for family, and sometimes, those don't overlap.

A profound sense of loneliness settled over me as I backed out of the Hadziahmetovic family circle, knocking me into a big funk. Watching the Hadziahmetovics made my thoughts drift to my own unique and loving family. The bummed-out mood coupled with a tidal wave of shame over the way I'd been skulking around for the past several months, doing things I'd never even considered doing before.

Mom and Dad had always accepted me for exactly who I was, and I felt terrible for having tried to change into a different person. Trying to be someone other than myself was stupid, even with a great motivation, such as catching the attentions of a guy like Ismet. The sad fact was, even though I'd gone against my beliefs and my family's rules to fill my mind with television and pop culture about which I couldn't care less, in the end, none of it had made Ismet like me.

And it hadn't made *me* like me. Not one bit.

Seeing Ismet dote on his little sister that evening was probably the first time I'd ever really glimpsed the real Ismet. He wasn't trying to fit some American ideal for once. He was just being Ismet Hadziahmetovic— plain and simple. Man, I really liked the real him, and realizing that made me recognize with a jolt that I really liked the real me, too. I'd veered so far off the path of my life, trying so hard to be someone I thought Ismet wanted me to be, that I'd completely forgotten how great it felt to just be the girl my parents had raised. Thoughtful, introspective, easygoing, self-accepting, and open to others.

Svuda podji svojoj kuci dodji.

Those odd foreign words really meant something to me now. I definitely felt like I'd traveled the world over, like I'd journeyed far from who I really was, who I *wanted* to be. It was, indeed, time to go home.

I slipped out the front door of the Hadziahmetovics' house and stopped for a moment on the porch. Snowflakes so big they reminded me of white, lace doilies fluttered down and melted on my skin. I couldn't see my beloved stars tonight, but I knew they were there. They were always there, just like family.

The day's events had winnowed down all the dreck of junior year until I could see the truth clearly for the first time in months. I didn't want to be the perfect pop-savvy teenager to win a great guy, or for any other reason. I wanted to be Just Meryl, the girl who knows way too many boring facts and isn't afraid to share them. The girl who wears clothes because they're comfortable, not because they're in style. The girl who FINALLY knows who Buffy is, but doesn't freakin' care.

THAT was me.

If and when some guy was smart enough to value all the facets of my admittedly quirky personality, then swell. I'd have a boyfriend. Until then, I was perfectly fine with being Meryl Morgenstern, the unhip girl who'd once been mistaken for a subsistence farmer.

I jumped into the Volvo with a smile on my face, more than ready to move on from the past few months. I didn't want to go back into the house and tell the Hadziahmetovics good-bye right then, but I figured they had enough on their minds anyway. They wouldn't even miss me. I would call tomorrow and check on Jenita's condition and say hello.

For the first time since the night Shefka had told me what kind of girls Ismet yearned to attract, I actually felt okay being alone and dateless.

There was another Bosnian phrase I'd learned that suddenly popped my head: *Ne sij tikve di jos nisu nikle.* It meant, "Don't plant pumpkins where they never sprouted."

Duh!

I'd planted and planted and planted hopes and wishes and dreams all year long, always in the same field (Ismet's), and always with bad results. It was high time I started looking for a new plot of land.

I'd be a liar if I said I didn't feel a pang of regret about Ismet, but I was done sowing seeds in a fallow field. Maybe I'd take a break from planting altogether, get my world back on track. Next time, I'd pick something easier to grow . . . like a second head!

I'd been home for about an hour, and I'd just gone up to my room to send an email to Lila and Caressa when I heard unfamiliar voices downstairs. Unfamiliar, that is, until I strained a little to make out the words.

My heart leapt. Ismet?

Curiosity warred with shock inside me, but for some reason, I didn't run immediately downstairs to find out why he was at my house. When I'd left his place, he'd been ensconced in the family fold taking care of his sister. In fact, that was where he should be right this minute.

Why WAS he here? On tonight of all nights.

I had to know.

As quietly as I could, I crept to the top of the staircase and sat down. Ismet was engaged in polite small talk with my mother while they waited for my father to join them. When he finally did, my parents invited Ismet into the living room. From my vantage point, I could see them through the balusters, but they couldn't see me. Perfect.

"What brings you out on a snowy night like this, young man?"

"It is Meryl, sir."

My nerves zinged, and I covered my mouth with both hands to hold in the squeak that wanted to emerge. For a few moments I went bonkers with excitement, but then I figured his parents probably sent him over to say thank you for my help or find out why I'd left without telling them, or something. That settled me down enough to listen calmly.

"Meryl told us what happened to your little sister. I trust she's okay?" Dad asked, clutching his pipe between his teeth. It was odd—I loathed cigarette smoke, but the scent of pipe tobacco felt safe and comforting to me, because it reminded me of Dad.

"She has a broken ankle, but that will heal. We are thankful to have found her. When I left, she was sleeping from the medication." He cleared his throat. "But, about Meryl."

"She's upstairs if you'd like me to run and get her."

I half stood, preparing to bolt if my mom headed this way.

"Not yet," Ismet told them, surprising me again. "I came to speak with you both."

Mom and Dad exchanged a look, then Dad asked, "What's on your mind?"

"Can I get you something to drink, Ismet?" Mom asked.

ARGH! I wanted to throw a pillow at her. Quit with the hospitality, already, Mom. LET THE GUY TALK! He was trying to get to the ME part, and I so wanted him to go there.

"No, thank you." Ismet stalled with a bit of fidgeting and throat clearing, but he finally looked at my father directly. "You see, I have been sort of blind to Meryl, although she and I are friends. I thought that I wanted . . . well, what I mean to say is I never noticed . . . what I would really like is permission to date your daughter."

My eyes bugged, and I took a risk and pressed my face to the space between the balusters. I wanted to make sure his words had been sincere and not some kind of a joke. They didn't appear to be. He looked like he meant it.

ISMET HADZIAHMETOVIC WANTED TO DATE ME!!

How? Why? When?

I forced my racing thoughts to still and just listened.

Ismet sat on the edge of one of my mom's leather club chairs. He wore a navy blue pea coat, unbuttoned, and he grasped his knit ski cap in both of his hands. He looked earnest and sweet and sooooooo totally adorable.

My parents must've thought so, too, because they shared one of those "Awwwww" smiles with each other before answering.

God, what if they said no?!

"We can't give you permission to date our daughter, Ismet," my dad said, bringing my worst fears to life.

I leapt to my feet and raked all ten fingers into the front of my hair. Did I just hear what I thought I heard? I was ready to hurl myself down the stairs and plead Ismet's case, when my dad surprised me by adding, "Only Meryl can decide if she wants to date you. But you do have our blessing to ask her."

Ismet visibly relaxed in his chair, and my shoulders dropped, too. I blew out a breath as my hands and knees trembled.

"Thank you. May I—" He glanced toward the stair-case and I backtracked so fast trying not to be seen, I knocked my calves on the top step and fell on my butt, right there on the landing. *Yeouch*. But, at least Ismet hadn't busted me.

"May I see her for a few minutes?"

"Of course, dear," my mom said. She stood and smoothed the front of her wool skirt. "Let me just run and get her."

And there it was, my cue to bolt. I sprinted back into my room, yanked a brush through my hair, chomped down a breath mint, and fluffed a little bronzer on my cheeks, all before my mom knocked. Before replying, I took a flying leap across the room and landed on my bed. I picked up a book, and I swear I looked and sounded totally nonchalant when I said, "Come in."

Mom cracked the door slightly and peered in, her smile big and her eyes shining. "Honey, Ismet is here to see you."

I feigned surprise. "In this weather?"

She nodded. "Perhaps you should come down."

"Okay," I said, with excitement. I couldn't fake the whole casual thing anymore. I walked over to my mom and we hooked arms.

"He's very cute," she whispered.

I giggled. "I know," I whispered back.

When we reached the bottom of the stairs, Ismet saw us and stood. He smiled at me in a way I'd only dreamed of before—as though he really saw me, and liked what he saw. "Hi, Meryl."

Yummmmmmmmmmmmy accent. "Hi."

"We'll just leave you two to talk, won't we, honey?" she said to my father.

"Absolutely."

He stood, then Mom said to Ismet, "It was so nice to visit with you. Please give our love to your little sister."

"Thank you," Ismet said.

"I do hope you'll be back."

Ismet gazed at me before telling my mom, "I hope so, too."

It was so romantic! SWOON!

After my parents had vacated the general vicinity, I tilted my head toward the heated sunroom at the front of the house. "Let's go out here."

I watched his Adam's apple jump a couple times, and I have to say it was a relief to know he seemed as nervous as I felt. The equal footing was a good thing, especially because I had some things to say to Ismet that weren't going to be easy.

Ismet followed me into the sunroom, and we took a seat side by side on the glider. Thick thermal windows ran along three walls of the room, opening up to views of the storm. The only light came in through the window into the house, as an ambient glow from the living room. We decided to leave it that way so we could watch the snow.

"I can't believe you're here on tonight of all nights, Ismet. How's Jenita?"

"Jenita is fine." He turned so he could face me, and for a few moments, he seemed to struggle with his segue into the meat of the conversation. "I went to look for you, Meryl, and you were gone."

I lifted one shoulder in a little shrug. "You needed some family time." Now was my chance. "And, if you want the truth, I needed some, too."

He pressed his lips together, then reached over and took one of my hands in both of his. His thumb brushed gently over my knuckles, and I could swear my heart had stopped. "I owe you an apology," he said.

"For what?"

"For . . ." He did this self-deprecating little mouth twist that made me melt. " . . . I guess for not treating you as kindly as you treated me."

"You've always been kind, Ismet."

"Yes, but——" He blew out this impatient breath. "Not in the way that . . . what I mean is . . . I just want you to know——" He broke off, swearing in Bosnian, which made me giggle. "Meryl, would you like to go out with me?"

I studied him for a few long moments. Part of me wanted to say yes immediately and forget the past few months, but I knew I needed to clear the air a bit. I wanted to start our dating relationship with everything out in the open. "I would love to go out with you, but only under a few conditions."

A small line bisected his forehead, just between his sandy brows. "Conditions?"

I nodded, feeling strong and determined. "You see, I've been trying to catch your attention for months." I paused, and he showed me the respect of not feigning surprise. "When I couldn't accomplish that by just being me, I did some things that weren't me. Things that made me feel like I was living a lie."

His eyes widened, almost imperceptibly. "Like what?"

I quickly told him about all my nights wasted sitting on the sales floor of Sears. As I related the tale, the whole POINT became crystal clear to me. Finding a boyfriend wasn't about trying to transform yourself into the perfect image of what you thought he wanted. It was about being exactly who you are and then finding a person who appreciated that. "I can't be someone I'm not, Ismet. I don't even want to."

"I know."

I held up a hand. "But, before I agree to go out with you, you need to know and respect that I will never be the most stylish or hip girl. I have no interest in watching television or going to movies." I shook my head. "I'll never choose that kind of passive entertainment over books or conversation or taking a hike through the woods."

He nodded.

I shrugged. "I don't want to be anyone other than who I am, Ismet. And if that means I'm not the right girl for you, I can make my peace with that and move on. I'm not hip."

Ismet did the sexy little mouth twist again. "In case you have not noticed, I am not hip either."

"I think you're kind of hip in an exotic, foreign kind of way."

He half smiled. "I thought I wanted to be hip in an

all-American kind of way, but I am finding it is easier to just be me."

We shared a grin.

"I want to go out with you because of the person you are, Meryl Morgenstern, not despite the person you are not. It just took me a while to figure that out."

"Shefka was right. You are clueless." I winked.

He laughed. "She said that?"

"Many times."

When the mood had grown serious again, Ismet gazed into my eyes like I had dreamed he would. "Meryl, you have been right there in front of me all this time, treating me well, being my friend, getting to know my family and my culture like no one else ever has. That means a lot to me, I have realized. And it will mean even more to me if we can go out sometime."

"One more condition," I told him, feeling bold.

He rolled his eyes playfully. "Gee, girls. Okay, name it."

"One of our dates must be going to junior prom." I bit my lip, hoping I hadn't pushed my demands too far.

He raised his eyebrows and looked utterly relieved. "Is that it?"

"Yes."

"Meryl, I would love to escort you to prom."

"Really?" Excitement welled up inside me, and part of me couldn't wait to get upstairs and email my friends with the news.

"Really. It is a date," he said. Then he lifted the back of my hand and brushed his lips against my knuckles.

DOUBLE SWOON! I almost passed out, seriously. Ismet's lips against my hand felt better than any kiss on the lips could ever feel.

At least, I imagined so, since I'd never been kissed.

But, now that I'd gotten a taste of romance, Ismet-style, I couldn't wait to experience that first lip kiss and judge for myself!

Sixteen

* ■ ■ * ■ ■ * ■ ■ *

caressa

Okay.

It's official.

I'm a complete and total, unredeemable idiot.

Oh, yes. Bobby Slade received the letter allegedly from my dad, and of course he'd responded. There isn't a blues musician alive who would turn down a collaboration opportunity with Tibby Lee. That's about on par with a singer passing up a chance to work with Carlos Santana. Uh, yeah, it JUST DOESN'T HAPPEN.

So, what I surmise is this: Bobby contacted my dad, who was duly confounded about the letter he'd never written. The two of them started talking, put the puzzle pieces together, concluded what had happened, and had a good-natured laugh about what a SILLY CHILD Tibby

Lee's daughter was (horrors). But then they got to talking and decided working together would be a good move after all, so Dad invited Bobby up to White Peaks to discuss ideas. Dad, however, simply couldn't pass up the chance to teach me a lesson, so he invited Bobby to just POP into my life without any warning whatsoever.

Ever heard of NATURAL CONSEQUENCES?

My dad is big on natural consequences. I'd put him in the awkward position of being caught unaware, and he repaid the favor big time.

ACKKKKKKKK!

If only he hadn't chosen opening week of *Beauty and the Beast* to teach me this all-important life lesson. But, GOD, had I ever learned. Bobby Slade was indisputably hot, but he was also . . . old. WAY older than the picture of him I had in my mind. I mean, not OLD old like my dad, but way too old for me, and I was so embarrassed. Why hadn't I seen our inherent incompatibility before I went and launched my career as the most gigantic village idiot ever? I was so humiliated and ashamed by what I'd done, I can't even tell you.

My two best friends had both scored their ultimate dream dates for prom, and all I'd scored was a gigantic ego blow. I'd be stuck at home painting my toenails on prom night, all because I'd stupidly fallen for some older guy on a CD case and I wouldn't listen to anyone tell me that was INSANE.

WAHHHHHHHHHHHH! Lila and Meryl had treated me like I'd gone off the deep end ever since my dumb supper revelations, and it was no wonder!

I'd spent the entire day freaking out, and the stress sent my poor vocal cords into some kind of weird spasm. Curtain time was a mere thirty minutes off, and the only sound I could make sounded like the mix between a gasp and a fake belch. No lie—not a single note would come out when I tried to sing. Still, Cabbiatti forced me to costume up and get ready to go on, because he thought I was faking it.

No matter how I tried to convince him, Cabbiatti didn't believe that I couldn't talk or sing without squawking. I think he suspected it was a cheap eleventh-hour plea to be taken out of the play and reassigned to the makeup crew, but please. Like I'd wait until OPENING NIGHT and sabotage the whole production. On the contrary, I had hoped I would deliver a standout performance now that Bobby Slade was in the audience, but it looked like I'd have to stand out *back* while the understudy played Belle.

Yay me—I got to doubly embarrass myself in front of a Grammy-winning hottie, all in a matter of two days.

I listened to the sounds of the orchestra tuning their instruments and my fellow singers warming up their voices and felt bleak. I tried to run through scales myself, to no avail.

I paced up to the curtains and peered out at the quickly filling auditorium as the panic bubbled up in my sore throat. Lila and Meryl sat dead center in the front row. I spied their families sitting a couple rows back, then I grimaced and scanned the audience for my family . . . and Bobby.

UGH, there they were, right in the front row but off toward stage right. My eyes misted over with tears, and I let the velvet curtain drop from my fingers. Sure, I hadn't wanted to be in this dumb musical, but I hated to let them down.

"Caressa."

I spun around to find the director looming over me. "Yeah?" I croaked.

Cabbiatti released a long-suffering sigh. "Look, if you

wanted to stage a revolt, you should've done it prior to opening night."

"But, I'm not—"

"You know, heart problems run in my family." He laid his palm on the left side of his chest. "You kids will be the death of me, I swear."

"I'm not faking it," I squeaked and gasped. "I absolutely can't sing, Mr. Cabbiatti." I spread my arms. "Why would I embarrass myself like this in front of the cast? Ninety-nine percent of the girls have been praying this entire time that I'd truly break a leg, you know. Would I give them that satisfaction?"

My raw, raspy monologue went a long way toward convincing him my throat problems were on the up and up. He planted his fists on his hips, took a deep breath in, then released it out his nose. "Sing the scales for me."

I touched my fingertips to my throat, took in a breath, and tried. My voice sounded like a cell phone breaking up. *Can you hear me now?* NOT GOOD!

Mr. Cabbiatti looked so crestfallen, my eyes filled with tears and spilled down my cheeks. "I'm sorry."

In a rare moment of opening night compassion, Cabbiatti squeezed my shoulder. "I am, too. I had a friend in college whose vocal cords would seize up on opening night sometimes. Stage fright."

I nodded. "Caroline Weller is a wonderful understudy. she'll do a great job in my place."

"If only you realized how good you are, Caressa," Cabbiatti said, shaking his head slowly. "If only you could hear what the rest of us hear. You'd know, then, that no one can ever quite replace you."

Strangely, considering my whole stance on the singing thing, The Crab's quiet words of praise boosted my spirits. Temporarily. Now that it had been settled and Caroline would open in my place, a profound feeling of disappointment draped over me. I scuffed back into the dressing room to remove my beautiful costume and the thick stage makeup. Mark, the humpbacked ET Beast, levered himself out of the makeup chair and shuffled over to me.

"Whaddup, Caressa?"

"I lost my voice," I chirp-whispered.

His eyes widened, then looked sad. "I'm sorry to hear that. You sound awful."

"I *feel* awful. In more ways than one."

"I'll bet."

"It'll come back," I assured him, although I had my doubts. "Maybe even before the show closes. Who knows?"

Mark popped his hand out of the beast claw and held up crossed fingers. "Rest your vocal cords, Caressa. I'd like to act in at least one performance with you."

"I'll try." I wrapped my arms around him and patted the misshapen hump on his back. "Break a leg, Mark-o."

He pulled out of the embrace and winked. "I'll do it just for you." He leaned in. "Hopefully I'll break off this stupid hump, too. What's with this costume?"

We both laughed then, although I sounded like a dying frog. I just wanted the night to be over.

"I'm such a freak show!" I croak-wailed to my pals as Meryl drove me home from the theater and Lila came along for moral support. My dad had wanted me to ride home with him, Mom, and Bobby Slade, but I couldn't bear to. I think he could see in my eyes that I'd learned my lesson and needed a reprieve, because he told me to be careful and take my time. "How can I face him?"

Meaning Bobby, not my dad.

I felt like I owed him an explanation and probably an

apology, too, but my mortification felt too fresh. If only he'd leave and come back in a month. Maybe by then I would have stopped reeling enough to express my remorse without busting into hot tears of shame.

Lila leaned up from the back seat and squeezed my shoulder. "Can I say, despite how much this all sucks, I'm just glad you finally realized he's wrong for you?"

I leaned back against the headrest and tried to groan, but it came out more like a gargle. "Yes. Fine. Say it. I know I deserve it."

"It's okay," Meryl said. She reached over and patted my knee. "You were just being yourself. We've all made mistakes throughout this ordeal."

"That's for sure," Lila said, "probably starting with agreeing to that dumb supper!"

"Oh, be quiet, Lila," Meryl said, playfully.

"But, it all worked out for you two," I croaked.

Neither Lila nor Meryl denied this. I felt like the red-headed simpleton stepchild of the bunch, no offense to Meryl who WAS redheaded, but neither simple nor a stepchild. "What am I going to say to him?"

"Just speak from your heart."

I glanced over at Meryl, trying to absorb some of her

quiet confidence. I knew I HAD to apologize to Bobby Slade, but I honestly didn't even know how to start. "I wish you could wear a Caressa costume and do this for me, Mer."

She flicked me a quick smile, but turned her attention immediately back to the roads, which were still icy and snowpacked in places. Sometimes it was so obvious that her dad was the driver's ed teacher. Not that this was a BAD thing while navigating sketchy mountain roads.

"You can't be faulted if you're honest and you speak from the heart, Caressa," Meryl said. "You're sixteen. Teenagers make mistakes every day."

"She's right," Lila said. "And, if the speaking-from-the-heart option flops, pass the buck big time, girlfriend. Blame anyone and everyone but yourself."

"Lila!" Meryl glared at her in the rearview mirror. "We're all trying to correct our errors, *remember*?"

"Hey, I was only joking. But . . . it *could* work."

I smiled at Lila over the back of the seat. We hadn't come up with any solutions, but my pals had at least bolstered my confidence. All that dissipated when Meryl drove out of the portico, with a friendly little tap on her horn and a wave. I stood there alone in the silence, desperate to avoid going into the house at all.

But I couldn't.

With a deep breath, I pushed open the front door. I stopped in the entryway and listened; the muffled sounds of a jam session drifted out to me from Dad's recording studio. I was sort of relieved that Mom, Dad, and Bobby weren't waiting for me in the living room like judge, jury, and executioner. Feeling a tiny speck of hope, I dropped my purse and duffel bag, then hung my coat in the closet.

Now or never.

I wiped my palms on the sides of my jeans and made my way down the hallway to the studio. I knocked as lightly as humanly possible, hoping they wouldn't hear me and I could skulk away forever, but no such luck.

"Come in."

I opened the door. My gaze met Bobby's briefly, but I yanked it away. "Hi," I croaked.

"You sound plain awful, *chérie*. How do you feel?"

"Terrible," I said. Understatement.

My dad crossed the room and felt my forehead and cheek. It was such a sweet, almost momlike thing to do.

I smiled at him. "I'm going to go see about some honey tea for your throat. You visit with Bobby while I'm gone," he said pointedly. So much for a natural segue.

The studio door opened, then shut behind my retreating dad with a slam that sounded like a prison gate locking. I jumped, clenching my fists at my sides. After a moment, I released a breath and smiled tremulously at Bobby.

He smiled back, and he looked pitying. Was it because of my stupidity? UGH!!

"Sorry about your voice, Caressa. You must be disappointed to have missed opening night."

Man, was he hot. "Yeah." I tried to clear my throat, but it made me cough. When the bout ended and I was certain I hadn't hacked up a lung on the floor, I sank onto the edge of the sofa that ran along one wall of the studio. "Um . . . Bobby, I wanted to say . . . I'm sorry." Perched on the edge of my seat, I tried to follow Meryl's advice to speak from the heart. Really, what other choice did I have?

He set his guitar aside and crossed the studio to sit on the couch beside me. "For what?"

"For . . . you know." *Sure, make me say it out loud.* "For

tricking you." I flicked him a furtive, embarrassed glance beneath my lashes, then refocused on my lap. "To get you up here. I'm sure it was awful calling my dad just to find out he'd never written that letter in the first place."

"Not so bad, actually."

His words brought my head up, and my eyes went round with surprise. "Really?"

He shrugged. "Was being a little embarrassed worth it in order to meet Tibby Lee? Hell, yeah. And now look what's transpired."

"W-what?"

"He's going to produce my next single."

Shock zinged through me. "He is?"

"Yep." He leaned in and lowered his voice to a conspiratorial purr. "If you think about it, Caressa, I actually owe you."

I crinkled my nose, but my spirits lifted. "You aren't mad then? To have been lured up to Colorado by deluded jailbait?"

Bobby barked a laugh. "No. It's all good, Caressa. No harm, no foul."

I blew out a breath of relief. "Thank God."

"But tell me something."

"What?"

"How did the whole thing come about?"

ACK! *Ladies and Gents, welcome to White Peaks' production of "Hello, I'm a Dumbass," starring Caressa Thibodoux.* I gulped back my mortification and gave him the glossed-over, *Reader's Digest* version of the dumb supper and the events that followed. I could feel my face and neck grow hotter the more I explained. "The thing is, we were really just trying to find dates for junior prom, and it all got out of hand."

He crossed one ankle over the opposite knee. "Prom, huh? Believe me, I can see how that would be a motivation." He rubbed his jawline with the back of his knuckles. "You know, I never got to attend either of my proms."

"Why not?" Surely girls would have paid hard, cold cash to go to prom with the lethally hot Bobby Slade.

"Well, work, I guess. I released my first album when I was sixteen." He made a regretful face. "By the time prom rolled around, I was working long hours in the studio. No time to go."

Wow. I hadn't thought of that at all. "That sucks." I hunched my shoulders up and then relaxed them on a sigh. "But, it looks like I'll be in the same boat, except without the excuse of working."

"Tell you what." He dipped his chin and studied me. "You and I both know I'm way too old for you, right? We're on the same page there?"

"Uh, yeah. Totally." God, KILL ME NOW.

"But, I'd still like to know what it's like to attend a prom."

My throat tightened, and I blinked up at him in disbelief. Was he saying—?

"How about—as a thank you for hooking me up with your pops—how about I fly back up here and escort you to your prom."

The world stopped.

My heart stopped.

Thankfully, my bladder function also stopped.

Had Bobby Slade just asked me to prom?

"Are you kidding me?"

He grinned. "Not at all. It won't be a date, of course, because—"

"You're too old for me. I know."

He chuckled. "Exactly. But, I'll escort you. As friends. Deal?" He held out his hand for me to shake.

I reached up with trembling fingers and tucked my hair behind my ears. "I'd love that, Bobby. But I don't know if my parents will go for it."

"Relax. I'll ask your dad. It'll be fine." He thrust his hand a little closer. "So, deal?"

I broke into the hugest grin ever, then shook his hand. "Deal. I'd love to go to prom. As friends."

"Friends. Always."

After that, I chilled out enough for us to have a real conversation. I asked him about his music, and he asked me about my career aspirations. I confided in him about how hard it was to deal with everyone's expectations that I'd follow in my dad's footsteps. "I don't want to be a singer," I told him. "Regardless of the fact that I have the skills, it's just not what I want to do."

"What *is* your dream, Caressa?"

I didn't want to sound like the ultimate dreamer, but I felt so close to Bobby, I didn't want to lie. "I want to be a makeup artist on Broadway."

He nodded decisively, and he didn't even act like I was dreaming way too big. "Then do it, girl. Go for it with every ounce of your passion."

"You think so? You think I could actually do it?"

"Heck yeah. Take it from me. You can do anything you believe you can do." He leaned in, lowering his voice. "And forget the singing if it's not your thing. The only dreams worth living are those you feel passionate about. I come from a family of surgeons, and it was always expected that I'd toe the Slade family line and go to medical school, too."

"Did you ever want to become a doctor?"

He shook his head and cringed. "Blood makes me dizzy."

That cracked me up. "Singing makes me tired. But makeup brings me alive."

"Listen to your own words. Go forth and paint, Caressa. Follow your passion, and everything else will fall into place."

I smiled at Bobby and knew, without a doubt, that fate hadn't been wrong leading me to him. Not because we were destined to fall in love, but because I needed to hear the things he had to say.

And hey, I had an escort to prom!

Not just ANY escort, but the supersexy BOBBY SLADE.

Rock on!

epilogue
★★★*★★*★

The three of us were looking so freakin' babe-a-licious in our prom dresses, we couldn't tear ourselves away from the mirror. Meryl's was jade green taffeta, mine was red satin, and Caressa's was a goddesslike champagne-colored silk (it looked like a dress Nicole Kidman would wear to the Oscars—no lie!). Pair the dresses with Caressa's skilled makeup jobs, and I don't think any of us had ever felt so gorgeous before.

Our dates were expected at any moment when my dad knocked on the bathroom door. "Girls?"

"Yeah, Dad."

"Come on out so I can get some pictures before the guys arrive."

We all started mugging in front of the mirror, acting

like high-fashion models. "Vogue, Vogue—strike a pose," I told my pals. We busted into gales of laughter; quickly stuffed our evening purses with lipsticks, breath mints, little cameras, and other important items; and then strutted out to the living room. My dad snapped photos until we all started to whine, and then he told me, "Lila, I'd like to speak to you in the kitchen for a moment."

I stifled a groan. Here it came. The obligatory no drinking, no sex, no *blah blah blah*, no FUN speech. And just when I was feeling so happy and excited.

I followed my dad into the kitchen and leaned my back against the counters, watching him with a droll look on my face. I would've crossed my arms, but I didn't want to mess up my dress. "Okay, what's up, Dad?"

He crossed his arms and smiled at me. "You look so lovely, Lila Jane. It makes my heart hurt. You look so much like your mother when she was young."

A burst of pleasure made me look away. "Thanks." I wanted to lighten the mood, because the sudden realization that Mom couldn't be here for my very first prom night sort of bummed me out. "But, don't you want to give me your stern fatherly speech before the guys get here?"

"Speech?" My dad frowned. "That's not why I called you in here."

Huh? "Oh. What, then?"

"I wanted to give you this." He reached into his back pocket, extracted his wallet, and unfolded it. I thought at first that he was giving me money, which ruled in any situation. Imagine my surprise when he pulled out a brand spankin' new Colorado driver's license and passed it over. It even had my good picture on it!

My jaw dropped, and I gaped at the license for a few moments before grinning at my father. "Why . . . when—?"

"You earned it, Lila. I'm so proud of you."

"Still?" I curled my fingers around the license, loving the feel of it in my hand.

"Always."

"So, then—"

"Don't ask me about the car, my dear daughter."

I was so happy, I didn't even pout. Instead, I laughed and threw my arms around Dad's neck. "I love you, Daddy."